KU-353-219

SPECIAL MESSAGE TO READERS

This book is published by

THE ULVERSCROFT FOUNDATION,

a registered charity in the U.K., No. 264873

The Foundation was established in 1974 to provide funds to help towards research, diagnosis and treatment of eye diseases. Below are a few examples of contributions made by THE ULVERSCROFT FOUNDATION:

* ★ A new Children's Assessment Unit at Moorfield's Hospital, London.
* ★ Twin operating theatres at the Western Ophthalmic Hospital, London.
* ★ The Frederick Thorpe Ulverscroft Chair of Ophthalmology at the University of Leicester.
* ★ Eye Laser equipment to various eye hospitals.

If you would like to help further the work of the Foundation by making a donation or leaving a legacy, every contribution, no matter how small, is received with gratitude. Please write for details to:

THE ULVERSCROFT FOUNDATION,
The Green, Bradgate Road, Anstey, Leicestershire, LE7 7FU. England.
Telephone: (0533) 364325

Love is
a time of enchantment:
in it all days are fair and all fields
green. Youth is blest by it,
old age made benign: the eyes of love see
roses blooming in December,
and sunshine through rain. Verily
is the time of true-love
a time of enchantment—and
Oh! how eager is woman
to be bewitched!

TO BE LOVED

Andrew married the woman he had always loved despite the knowledge in his heart that Sarah married him for reasons of her own. He was patient and considerate but Sarah could not be loyal, and at last Andrew was forced to admit that another man possessed her heart. So much heartache could have been avoided if only he had known how vital it was to be loved . . .

Books by Lynne Collins
in the Ulverscroft Large Print Series:

REBEL NURSE
THE GOLDEN KEY
TO BE LOVED

LYNNE COLLINS

TO BE LOVED

Complete and Unabridged

ULVERSCROFT
Leicester

First published in Great Britain in 1961 by
Wright & Brown, Ltd.,
London

First Large Print Edition
published October 1990

British Library CIP Data

Collins, Lynne, *1933–*
    To be loved.—Large print ed.—
    Ulverscroft large print series: romance
    I. Title
    823'.914

ISBN 0-7089-2292-9

Published by
F. A. Thorpe (Publishing) Ltd.
Anstey, Leicestershire
Set by Rowland Phototypesetting Ltd.
Bury St. Edmunds, Suffolk
Printed and bound in Great Britain by
T. J. Press (Padstow) Ltd., Padstow, Cornwall

1

SARAH drove furiously along the dark country lanes, regardless of the blinding rain which hurled itself against the windscreen of her car, taking corners at breakneck speed but careless of the risks while her rage lasted. Her slim hands rested lightly but capably on the steering-wheel: her auburn curls were almost hidden by the multi-coloured scarf she had tied about her hair; her cool, grey eyes bored through the rain and the darkness, alert for familiar turns of the road. She looked calm but inwardly she seethed: when the anger faded, she would know a desperate hurt and bewilderment and she knew herself well enough to be sure that she could drive safely in anger but not if she was consumed with searing pain and disappointment.

The small sports car ate up the miles, and within an hour of leaving the bright lights of London, she turned into the long drive of Kendrick House. The big manor-house was situated on a hill overlooking the quiet, peaceful village of Avering. A few lights still burned in the windows despite the lateness of the hour.

Sarah garaged her car and hurried through the rain and wind to the house. She ran up the steps, searching for her doorkey in her handbag. As she let herself into the wide hall with its sweeping staircase and marble-paved floor, Andrew Whitaker came out of the library. He paused at the sight of her. "Hallo, Sarah. I didn't think you'd be back tonight," he said lightly.

"Oh, Andrew! I'd forgotten you were dining here. Had a good time?" She threw the words at him carelessly. She stripped off her gloves and shrugged her shoulders out of the heavy coat she wore. She pulled the scarf from her hair and leaned forward to regard her reflection in a hall mirror. She ran a hand lightly through her curls and shook her head to loosen them after the restricting effect of the scarf.

"Yes, thanks. I was just about to make my way home," Andrew told her.

She met his gaze in the mirror. Her eyes narrowed slightly as a thought crossed her mind suddenly. "Have a drink with me before you go?" she invited. Sensing his hesitation, she added swiftly, sharply: "Please yourself—I don't mind drinking alone, you know."

He smiled. He knew Sarah too well to take offence at her tone or the words. "Isn't it a little late?"

"It is, if you think so. But I'm going to have a drink, anyway. It's a foul night and I need one after driving from Town in such weather." She crossed the hall to the drawing-room.

"Your father is in the library," Andrew informed her.

"Let's leave him in peace, shall we? I want to talk to you, Andrew—without an audience."

He raised an eyebrow. "Very well. Ten more minutes can't make much difference."

She turned to throw him an exasperated glance. "Must you be so conservative? Because it happens to be almost twelve o'clock, you think you must leave before the witching hour strikes. What I have to say might easily take longer than ten minutes—but if you're more interested in the conventions . . ."

He interrupted. "You are in a foul mood, Sarah." He walked across to her and opened the door of the drawing-room. "I gather you didn't enjoy your evening."

She preceded him into the room. "I don't want to talk about my evening, thank you." She went over to the fireplace and replenished the dying fire with a log from a basket that was kept by the side of the hearth. She kicked it viciously into place and a shower of sparks flew up the wide chimney. "Brandy, please, Andrew."

He poured the drinks and joined her with the glasses in his hands. She took her drink from him and stood looking down at it for a few moments, turning the glass between her slim fingers. Always at home and fully at his ease, Andrew sat down in a comfortable armchair and crossed one leg over the other. He studied her thoughtfully and wondered what had happened to put her into such a bad temper. He had known Sarah for a good many years and he had seen her in every mood: he was extremely fond of her and they were good friends; at intervals during the last few years he had asked her to marry him but always she had refused and now he had all but given up hope that they might continue their long association as man and wife.

"I'm ready to listen," he prompted her quietly. She glanced at him and he realised that her anger had faded. Her moods were swift to change but it took him a moment to recognise the look which narrowed her beautiful eyes—then he knew that she was carefully considering some new idea.

"Don't rush me—I'm thinking," she replied slowly.

He smiled. Raising his glass, he said: "Well, here's to the future!" It was a toast which she associated with him and at that moment it fitted in remarkably well with her thoughts.

She drank with him but did not repeat his words. Placing her empty glass on a low table, she sank to her knees before the fire. Holding out her hands to the blaze, she said: "I suppose you have plenty of plans for the future, Andrew?"

He shrugged. "One or two. Why?"

She turned her head to smile at him.

"Once your plans for the future included me—have you changed your mind now?"

He straightened quickly. "I'm still of the same mind, Sarah."

"Do you think it would work out?" she asked and there was a faint note of hopelessness in her voice.

Not wishing to appear too eager to seize on the implications of her words, he shrugged. "We'd stand as much chance as most people, I imagine," he returned lightly. "But you wouldn't marry me, my dear."

Again that swift turn of her auburn head. "I might."

He held her gaze firmly. "What about David Montrose?"

Her glance wavered slightly. "To hell with David Montrose!"

He pulled thoughtfully at his lip. "I see. So things didn't work out as you hoped, Sarah. But it isn't like you to turn to me as a balm for your hurt feelings. I thought you were more confident that there's always someone waiting round the next corner."

She ran an impatient hand through her hair. "I can't spend my whole life looking round corners. Andrew. I want to get married . . ."

"And it doesn't matter very much which man you choose to marry? Is that how you feel?" He carefully hid the pain which her careless words gave him.

"Oh, Andrew—must you make it all so difficult? I thought you wanted to marry me."

"So I do—but not on those terms." He spoke firmly and finally.

She held out her hand to him. "Do you want me to pretend that I'm madly in love with you, Andrew? You've always been a stickler for honesty. Well, I'm being honest with you now. I'm very fond of you and we get on well together. I know we could be happy. I'd like to marry you."

He caught her hand and held it tightly. His grip was almost painful. "Sarah, this is ridiculous. You've had a row with Montrose tonight, driven home in a flaming temper—and now you want to marry me just to spite him. Do you think I'm a fool? I know the way your mind works, my dear."

"I haven't been with David tonight," she said stifly. "I haven't been out with him for weeks, if you must know. We were washed up a long time ago. David has nothing to do with my decision." Her eyes were suddenly pleading. "Marry me, Andrew—please marry me."

He drew her to him and cradled her face between his hands. "Why?"

"Because I'd never be happy with anyone but you," she said desperately. "I know you'll look after me—I know you love me, Andrew. I want to be safe and you're the safest person I know."

He clasped her in his arms and her face was against his shoulder. His cheek against her hair, his eyes were very thoughtful. Was it possible that Sarah really loved him despite everything? That cry had come from her heart and he felt that she had never been more sincere. She might not even understand her own feelings, but surely her instinct was guiding her to entrust her life to him. It would be so easy to deceive himself that she was in love with him; that she had always loved him but had always lacked the perception to realise her feelings; but he must not take the easy way out. Andrew Whitaker had never been a man to take the easy way out of anything.

"Sarah," he whispered against her hair. "I wish I knew what to do. I love you and I'd willingly marry you tomorrow if I thought it was the right thing. But I can't marry you when I know that you don't love me. Too much is involved, my darling. You might be happy for a few months—until you find a man you really can love . . ."

She pulled away and pressed her mouth to his, stemming the flow of words. There was an urgency in the fierce pressure of her lips which fired passion and momentarily quelled his doubts. Maybe she was wiser than he realised. Maybe she should marry him and perhaps love would come in time.

"Don't let me down, Andrew," she murmured against his lips. "I've always been able to turn to you. We will be happy —I know we will. I'll never look at another man, I promise. Andrew, Andrew, you must marry me!"

He released her and rose abruptly to his feet. He began to pace the floor, hands thrust deep into his pockets, a frown creasing his brow. He was a tall man, powerfully built with broad shoulders and massive chest which fined down to a surprisingly slim waist and hip-line. His dark hair was crisp and sprung vitally from his temples. His dark eyes and bronzed skin gave him a somewhat sombre look but he was handsome and reassuring and very masculine.

Sarah leaned against the armchair, watching him, her eyes anxious. It was vitally important that he should agree to her request. She knew that she did not love him, knew that she never would—but she firmly believed at that moment that her only chance of real happiness lay with him.

"Andrew?" she said tentatively.

He swung round. "I can't," he said fiercely. "I can't, Sarah."

"But you love me! You do still love me, don't you?"

"I love you too much!"

She was on her feet in a moment. She ran into his arms, held him close, pressed her slim body urgently against him. "Hold me, Andrew—hold me!" she begged.

His arms tightened involuntarily about

her and he bit his lip against the fierce
desire to snatch at the happiness she
offered. How long would such happiness
last? How long would her determination to
be a good wife to him last? How long
would she find happiness with him?

Suddenly the drawing-room door
opened and Frances Kendrick, Sarah's
cousin, entered the room. She paused in
surprise. "I'm sorry," she said lamely. "I
thought Travers had forgotten to switch
off the lights . . ."

Sarah turned to her cousin, her eyes
blazing suddenly. "Frances—Andrew and
I are going to be married!"

The words of denial were on his lips but
he choked them down. Perhaps her way
was the only way. She had forced him into
a position where he could not refuse
now to marry her—and Frances had un-
wittingly played into her hands.

Frances stared at them—and then
Andrew released Sarah from his arms.
"Are you serious?" she stammered and
then realised the inanity of her words. "I
don't know what to say," she said with a
little, forced laugh.

"Sarah shouldn't have sprung the news

on you so abruptly," Andrew said quietly. "But is it such a shock, Frances?"

She met his eyes levelly. "No. I think I've always known that Sarah would eventually marry you, Andrew." She moved swiftly, impulsively, to kiss Sarah's cheek. "Be happy, Sarah," she said gently. Then she turned to give Andrew her hand. "Congratulations!" Again that quiet little laugh. "Am I the first to know?"

Sarah nodded. "Yes."

Frances smiled. "You've timed your engagement well—Uncle John will be delighted to announce it at your birthday ball next week, Sarah." She walked to the door. "I expect you have a lot to discuss so I'll say goodnight."

The door closed quietly behind her. Sarah looked at Andrew almost fearfully, hesitantly. "Are you furious?" she asked.

"I should be," he said. "But now that the die is cast . . ." He shrugged. "That was one way of making up my mind, Sarah."

"You won't regret it," she promised fervently. She moved close to him, slipped her arms about him and lifted her face. "Kiss me, Andrew."

Tenderly, he sought her lips. His kiss was light, gentle—but she pressed her body against him and her lips were urgent and demanding beneath his. Despite himself, he found himself thinking that it was almost as though she wished to drown the memory of another man's kisses, another man's nearness, in his embrace and again he knew the stirring of unease.

He released himself and took a cigarette case from his pocket. Inserting a cigarette between his lips, he ignited a table lighter and drew deeply on the soothing nicotine of the cigarette.

Sarah was puzzled by his abrupt withdrawal. She studied him for a moment. Then she held out her hand for a cigarette and he opened his case once more with a word of apology. She bent her head over the flame of the lighter. "What's wrong, Andrew?" Now that she had forced the issue, she was composed again, in control of her emotions, prepared to accept the inevitable that she had brought upon herself.

He did not attempt to prevaricate. "I don't like the feeling that you're trying to simulate passion when you kiss me, Sarah.

I know that you don't love me—and you know it, so don't pretend. I'll marry you on your terms, as you seem to want it so much—but don't carry on a deception with me."

She flushed. "I'm sorry." She did not try to excuse her actions. She should have known that Andrew knew her too well, that he could not be deceived, that her kisses must seem as empty to him as they were to her. If only they were not empty! If only she could know joy in his embrace, swift ecstasy in his kisses!

He touched her cheek with a gentle forefinger and smiled at her. Then he walked to the fireplace. "I wonder if your father is still up," he said casually. "Shouldn't we break the news to him?"

"Frances has probably already done just that," Sarah returned with a shrug.

"In that case, we should join him and talk things over."

"Isn't it a little late?" she asked. "Time enough for discussions tomorrow, surely?"

"As you wish." He threw his half-smoked cigarette into the fire. "I must go home, Sarah. But I'll be here about eleven

—I'll drive you to Town so that we can choose your engagement ring."

She bit her lip at the finality of the words. Once he had placed a ring on her finger, there could be no going back. But she did not want to retract. She would marry Andrew and be safe for the rest of her life.

When he had gone, she walked slowly up the wide staircase to her bedroom, her hand trailing on the polished balustrade. She was committed to marry Andrew and there could be no uncertainty with regard to her future.

Frances crossed the hall in her dressing-gown and paused at the sight of Sarah. "Has Andrew gone?"

"Yes. He's coming tomorrow morning. We're going to Town to choose the ring." She went into her room and Frances followed her.

The two girls were not alike yet a close scrutiny betrayed the family resemblance. Frances' father had been John Kendrick's brother: her parents had died in a car crash when she was a mere child and she had lived at Kendrick House ever since as one of the family. Sarah's auburn beauty tended to overshadow her cousin's quiet claims to good looks but Frances had her own appeal with the soft chestnut of her long hair which she usually wore coiled in a chignon at the nape of her neck and the soft grey-blue of her eyes with the long, velvety lashes.

"He must be very happy that you've decided to marry him at last," Frances said quietly.

Sarah sat down at her dressing-table and began to cream the make-up from her lovely face. "He's been asking me for years," she said carelessly.

"Yes, I know. You made up your mind quickly, Sarah."

Sarah's eyes narrowed sharply. "Why do you say that? How do you know that I didn't tell Andrew a long time ago that I'd marry him?"

Frances smiled. "Because we see a great deal of Andrew and I feel sure he would have made some mention of it."

Sarah continued with the creaming. "I suppose you've seen more of him lately than I have."

Frances took the remark personally as she knew she was meant to do. "I'm at home more than you are," she returned gently.

"You're fond of Andrew, aren't you?" Sarah asked carelessly.

"Of course. We all are. He's one of the family already." She moved about the room, tidying up the clothes and oddments which Sarah had left scattered before she went out for the evening. "Uncle John and Aunt Helen will be delighted that you're going to marry Andrew, after all."

"I thought you'd probably told Daddy already."

"He'd gone to bed," Frances returned. "In any case, I knew you'd want to break the news yourself. When I left you, I came straight up here." She put the books beside the bed straight and turned down the covers neatly. "Shall I run your bath?"

"I can't be bothered to bath now," Sarah replied. "I'm so tired I could sleep for a week. Don't worry, Frances." She rose from the stool and began to unzip her dress. She smiled at her cousin. "Thanks for tidying up—I left it in a state, didn't I? I really shouldn't let you wait on me so much."

Frances went to her assistance and

17

carefully lifted the elegant black dress over Sarah's head. She placed it on a hanger and slipped the dress into its place inside the long wall wardrobe. Sarah was suddenly irritated by her cousin's ministrations.

"Why don't you go to bed, Frances," she said, trying to keep the edge out of her tone. "I can manage now."

She obediently went to the door. "Goodnight, Sarah. Sleep well."

"Goodnight." As soon as the door was shut, Sarah sank down on the edge of her bed and rubbed her throbbing temples. It was a blessed relief to be alone. But with the solitude came back the pain and bewilderment—and she clung to the thought of Andrew to erase the need for David. Andrew loved her. Andrew would look after her. Andrew would protect her from further pain.

She stripped off her flimsy undergarments, pulled a sheer nightgown over her head and slipped between her bed-covers. She switched off the light and burrowed down into the comforting darkness—but David's beloved face was before her eyes and memory would not allow her to forget so many things which were linked with him. She tossed and turned restlessly, fighting the tears—but they won the battle and when she finally fell into a dream-filled sleep, her cheeks were wet and there was little ease in oblivion . . .

2

THE big hall was suddenly hushed as Colonel John Kendrick mounted to the fourth stair of the wide, sweeping staircase and held up his hand for silence. All heads turned towards him, conversation ceased, the small orchestra—already warned—broke off in the middle of a lively tune.

He was a tall man with an imposing presence and a magnificent head of white hair. A ruddy face and bright but kindly blue eyes gave him a benevolent appearance. He was a well-known and much-loved personality in the County and many years of service in the army had given him a forceful air of command so that when he mounted the stairs and held up his hand, not one of his guests was ill-mannered enough to ignore his request for silence.

He beamed upon them all. "The announcement I am about to make will not come as any surprise to most of you," he said in a voice that could be heard with ease at the far end of the hall. "But it gives my wife and myself great pleasure and I know you will all share our happiness in the engagement of our daughter, Sarah, to one of our oldest friends, Andrew Whitaker." He turned towards the small group which stood at the foot of the staircase: his wife Helen, Sarah and Andrew, and Frances, standing a little to one side as though she was aware that her claim to being one of the family was not as concrete. "I should like to propose a toast —to Sarah and Andrew." He raised the glass he held and instantly a chorus of voices repeated the toast. "We wish you both every happiness," he added when the tumult of sound had died down.

Sarah's hand was linked lightly in Andrew's arm. At her father's words, she exerted a slight pressure and he smiled down at her before he glanced up to nod his approval of the Colonel's words.

Andrew released himself from her clasp and stepped up to join the Colonel. In a few, well-chosen words he replied to the toast.

Several guests surged forward to offer congratulations and good wishes and the

Colonel patted him on the shoulder. "Better get back to Sarah—she's being overwhelmed," he said.

Andrew nodded. He looked down at Sarah, her slim body sheathed in a lovely dress of grey-green tulle, her auburn beauty outstanding as she smiled and laughed and prettily thanked her friends for their good wishes. He was as uncertain of the wisdom of this engagement now as he had been a week ago but there was no doubt that everyone else was highly delighted with the turn of events—and he had no real proof that Sarah regretted her decision. "Thank you, sir," he said, addressing the Colonel and the two men exchanged friendly glances of mutual understanding.

"You're the best man for her, Andrew," the Colonel said and then coughed as though he were embarrassed by the unexpected and unaccustomed revelation of his affection for the younger man. "I think you know how to handle her," he went on. "She's a high-spirited young filly."

Andrew smiled. "I don't think there's much I need to be told where Sarah is concerned, sir."

"No, of course not. You probably know her better than anyone else does. Quite frankly, I've never understood her thoroughly. I've always taken the easy way and given her her head—let her jump her own fences. Luckily she's never come to any harm. I'm satisfied now—I needn't worry about her any more." He nodded to Andrew. "I'd better not keep you any longer—Sarah will be getting restive."

Andrew returned to Sarah's side, still faintly amused by the Colonel's words. He invariably spoke of his daughter as though she were a thoroughbred horse whenever he was embarrassed or reluctant to discuss her actions.

The Colonel descended the staircase and immediately Frances moved towards him with a glass of champagne she had procured for him. He smiled down at his niece. "Well, was it all right?" he asked. It was strange that he was always at his ease with Frances and yet his own daughter had the power to stifle the expression of affection which he longed to demonstrate.

"Perfect," Frances assured him. She

23

laughed up at him. "So much for your claim that you were nervous!"

"That's one announcement I've never had to make before," he returned. He looked across to Sarah and Andrew. "They make a handsome couple," he said proudly. "I thought Sarah would eventually come to her senses and marry Andrew. I could never understand what she saw in that Montrose fellow!"

Frances shrugged. "Youthful infatuation," she suggested.

"I expect you're right." He frowned slightly. "You haven't a drink, my dear. Come along—we must remedy that. Let's see if we can fight our way through the crowd." A kindly hand at her elbow, he guided her through the motley gathering. As they passed, Frances glanced at Sarah. She was radiantly lovely, laughing at some quip and looking up into Andrew's face. Frances felt a small pang of envy but she swiftly repressed it.

The Colonel was pressed into conversation with friends and Frances stood alone for a few minutes in the doorway of the drawing-room. Her eyes instinctively sought the dark head of Andrew Whitaker.

Was he really happy about his engagement to Sarah? She could not rid herself of the feeling that something was lacking. Sarah did not have the radiant happiness of a girl in love and newly engaged: Andrew was too reticent. He had always been able to talk freely to her and they had become very close during the last year or so while Sarah had been more interested in a gay social round with her many friends—but since the evening when Sarah had blurted out the news of the engagement, Andrew had seemed strangely reluctant to discuss Sarah or the future with Frances.

Did he sense a similar reluctance in her to think of his eventual marriage to Sarah? Did he suspect the effort it was to behave as though she were delighted and happy about the engagement? Had he pierced her guard in that first brief moment when she walked into the drawing-room and found Sarah in his arms? If he was aware that she loved him, then Andrew would naturally be considerate of her feelings for he was not a man who enjoyed inflicting pain whether consciously or unconsciously.

Frances had known for a long time that

Andrew loved her cousin. She had reconciled herself to the knowledge for she had been convinced that Sarah would never marry him—and she had contented herself with Andrew's affectionate friendship, hoping that one day she might take Sarah's place in his thoughts and affections. It had been a shock to be told of Sarah's decision—and it had been even more of a shock to realise how deeply affected she was by it. She had always been a little in love with Andrew: now she realised that he was the only man she would ever love and it was not easy to accept the futility of her love. It was a constant struggle to conceal her feelings, to protect herself against the slightest piercing of the armour she had been forced to erect about her love, to fight against the feeling of anguish which assailed her when she saw Andrew and Sarah together, to pretend an interest in the plans that Sarah was already making for her wedding.

It seemed to Frances that her cousin was also playing a part: that having made up her mind to marry Andrew, she was determined that no one should suspect any lack of feeling on her part; she behaved like any newly-engaged girl, hanging on Andrew's every word, seeking his company at every possible moment, eagerly discussing wedding plans, revelling in the congratulations and good wishes and presents which were showered upon them both. To anyone who did not know Sarah as well as Frances did, it would appear that she was happy about her engagement—but Frances could not help wondering and doubting.

It was such a short time ago since David Montrose was the be-all and end-all of her existence—and Sarah had confided in Frances to a great extent where her hopes and dreams for the future were concerned. This sudden engagement to Andrew conflicted violently with those confidences —and Frances could not believe in her heart that Sarah's eyes had been abruptly opened to the fact that Andrew was the only man who could make her happy. Sarah was playing some strange game of her own—and Frances was angry when she thought that Andrew was merely being used as a pawn. It was not right to use a man's love as a weapon against another man! She had no proof—except her knowledge of Sarah and the way she had felt about David Montrose.

Surely Andrew must know that Sarah did not love him? He was not a fool to be deceived so easily by this abrupt show of affection. Surely he was not so much in love with Sarah that he was prepared to marry her on any terms? He was too intelligent to believe that true happiness could be found in such a marriage. Or did he hope that, once married to him, Sarah would learn to love him and he was willing to take the risks involved?

Frances told herself that a man—or a woman—in love would snatch at any straw and it was quite possible that Sarah had managed to convince him that he was the only man she had ever really loved. If so, surely she had the right to go to Andrew and tell him that she firmly believed that Sarah was still in love with David Montrose—but Frances knew that she could never do this. She could not interfere. Andrew was a man with a mind of his own and the right to make his own mistakes—and perhaps she was wrong and Sarah did love him.

As though he sensed her contemplation

and her thoughts, Andrew turned and met her eyes. He smiled warmly and indicated that she should join them. Frances turned away abruptly. She began to circulate about the big hall, attending to the needs of the guests, making introductions here and there, carrying out all the duties of hostess which invariably fell to her. Helen Kendrick had a reputation for being a wonderful hostess: very few people knew or suspected that it was Frances' careful planning and management and instinctive flair for such occasions which supported that reputation. Helen was well content to leave everything to her capable niece and to receive the compliments and thanks of her guests without a qualm of her conscience.

It was some time later that she turned to find Andrew at her elbow with a glass in his hand that he offered to her. "You're always too busy to enjoy yourself," he reproached her. "Forget everyone else for a few moments and have a drink and a cigarette."

She smiled. "I am enjoying myself," she returned but she took the glass and accepted the cigarette which he gave her.

Their hands touched as he supplied a light and a tiny, involuntary tremor ran through her slim body.

"It's been a very successful evening," he remarked. "Thanks to you!"

She demurred swiftly. "Oh no! I've done very little."

He laughed. Placing a hand on her slim shoulder, he exerted a gentle, affectionate pressure. "This is Andrew, remember," he teased. "You can't deceive me. I know very well that these affairs would be a terrible flop if you didn't keep an eye on everything. Helen never gives a thought to her guests—and the Colonel's always happy if he can take a few cronies and a bottle of whiskey into the library and forget everyone else."

"There always has to be one person who enjoys keeping an eye on things," Frances told him. Painfully aware of his clasp on her shoulder, she said quietly: "Shouldn't you be with Sarah?"

"I don't believe in dogging her every footstep," he returned. "She's talking to some friends." He nodded his head towards the group at the far side of the hall—a small group which was dominated by Sarah's looks and personality.

"She looks very lovely tonight," Frances said impulsively, sincerely.

Pride touched his eyes. "Yes, she does." He glanced down at Frances. "So do you, my dear," he added generously.

Emotion flooded her—warm appreciation of the compliment mingled with the conviction that he realised how overshadowed she was by Sarah and wanted to reassure her that her own looks would appeal to some men if he remained unmoved by them.

She moved away from him to stub out her cigarette in an ashtray. It gave her a few moments to recover her composure.

"You haven't said very much about my engagement to Sarah," he commented when she came back to his side.

She toyed with her glass. "There isn't much to say, Andrew. I'm pleased, of course—for your sake. I know you've always wanted to marry Sarah. But you must remember that it isn't really a surprise. After all, you and Sarah have been such good friends for a long time and you seem to understand her. She obviously realises now that she needs a man like you as a husband."

"Frankly, I'd given up hope," Andrew said honestly. "She seemed to prefer any man to me—and for over a year David Montrose monopolised her time and thoughts. I was surprised to learn that it's some time since she broke with him. I think she's had enough of flitting from romance to romance—and wants to settle down."

"Well, you have an excellent foundation for happiness," Frances said quietly. "Years of friendship and affection—and I think you know her very well, Andrew. I want you to be happy, anyway."

"Thank you, Frances." Unexpectedly, he stooped to brush her cheek with his lips. "I know you mean that, my dear."

She endured the kiss he bestowed upon her—but it took all her control to prevent herself from jerking away from that brotherly token of affection. She forced a smile to lips that were stiff. "I've neglected my duties long enough," she said, trying to speak lightly. "And you should go back to Sarah now—she's trying to attract your attention."

Andrew turned and met Sarah's imperative gaze. He was inwardly amused but pained by her recent display of possessiveness towards him. At least she did not attempt to deceive him when they were alone. Each knew exactly how matters stood. He did not seek to probe too closely into her reasons for wishing to marry him; he was a man in love and he wanted Sarah for his wife—but he could wish that he was marrying a woman who responded to his love with the same intensity of emotion. But no doubt they would make something of their marriage and he felt fairly confident that Sarah would be happy as his wife. He would do all in his power to ensure her happiness.

He excused himself from Frances and crossed the hall. Sarah linked her hand in his arm and smiled up at him. He looked down at the hand which lay so carelessly within the crook of his arm—the hand on which sparkled the diamond solitaire ring. Impulsively he laid his other hand over hers and pressed her fingers affectionately.

Momentarily, they stood alone among the crowd of friends and acquaintances who had been invited to the affair. "Am I overdoing it?" Sarah asked in a low tone.

He shook his head. "Not at all. You look happy—are you?"

"Of course!" Her voice held a note of surprise. "I know I'm doing the right thing, Andrew. I'll never let you regret it, either."

His eyes were very warm. "I won't regret it, Sarah."

"People have been asking me when we plan to be married, Andrew," she went on.

"What did you tell them?"

She shrugged prettily. "I said that there was no reason to wait—that we'd probably marry in a month or two."

He nodded. "Is that what you want?"

A shadow flitted briefly across her face. Then she smiled and said firmly: "Why not? We're going to be married—so why need we wait too long?"

He was silent for a moment or two. Then he said quietly: "You might change your mind yet, my dear. I think we should wait six months at least. I want you to be really sure about the future."

"I'm sure now," she said mutinously.

"Well, I'm not," he replied.

She threw him a startled glance. "What do you mean?"

"I'm not sure that you really know what you're doing," he explained. "I can't help thinking that you're only acting on impulse—an impulse which you'll regret when you've had more time to think things over."

"Oh, why won't you believe me?" she cried. "I want to marry you—and it isn't just an impulse. I've always meant to marry you, really."

"This is neither the time nor the place to discuss it, Sarah," he warned her as one of her many friends moved towards them.

She left the subject then but she looked at him with eyes that smouldered and he knew that later she would return to it. He stifled a faint resentment. If only their engagement and eventual marriage could be straightforward and uncomplicated! He was finding little happiness at the moment in the situation and he had no wish to argue constantly about the wisdom or otherwise of her decision.

Her friend was a late arrival and Sarah greeted him warmly. He had already learned of her engagement and she introduced him to Andrew. Formalities were exchanged then the man turned to Sarah. "I hope you don't mind, Sarah, but I dined with some friends and I couldn't shake them off when they found out I was coming on to a party."

"The more the merrier," Sarah assured him gaily.

"Come and meet them, won't you? I left them near the bar."

Sarah smiled at Andrew. "Will you excuse me, darling? Peter wants me to meet his friends."

He nodded. "I'll have a few words with Simon." He swung away and crossed over to an old friend who stood talking to Helen Kendrick.

Sarah looked after him then she linked her hand in Peter Joslin's arm. "Lead me to these friends who are so anxious to meet me," she told him lightly.

Peter grinned. "Two handsome men— so you'll be in your element . . ."

She laughed. "I have to watch my step now, Peter." She lifted her left hand so that the diamond flashed in the light.

"They're quite safe, I assure you." He

guided her through the press of people and into the drawing-room. A long bar had been set up and it was very busy at the moment. Peter looked about him for his friends. "There they are," he said and indicated two men who stood near the bar with their backs towards the door. Sarah allowed him to lead her across the room—then she stopped abruptly and pulled her hand from his arm.

"Peter! How could you!" she exclaimed furiously. His youthful face was puzzled. "What's wrong?"

"It's David!" she accused.

"Of course it is. I thought you'd be pleased to see him. It took a lot of persuasion to get him here, I can tell you."

Sarah looked about her desperately. "I can't possibly meet him!"

Even as the words left her lips, David Montrose turned and saw her. He smiled a welcome but his eyes were cold. Reluctantly Sarah moved towards him, her heart thudding, her blood icy in her veins—and the engagement ring she wore suddenly seemed to dominate the room . . .

3

HIS gaze ran over her and then bored deeply into her eyes. She quickly dropped her lashes to hide the joy she could not help feeling at sight of him. She managed to rescue the shreds of her composure and she lifted her chin proudly. He could never hurt her again. She was safe while she blazoned Andrew's ring on her finger. David must never know that he still had the power to flood her entire being with a tumult of emotion.

She held out her hand to him. "This is a surprise," she said lightly. "Nice to see you, David." The clasp of his strong fingers seared her flesh: the coldness of his brilliant blue eyes seared her heart. She knew a momentary triumph. The news of her engagement had shocked and pained him. So he had not thought her capable of carrying out her threat. But the triumph was swiftly followed by remorse. She had hurt him—and in doing so she had hurt herself. But she would not retract now.

Andrew was by far the better man—and she was committed. David's pride was hurt—not his heart. He had never really loved her.

"Peter has a persuasive tongue," he replied smoothly. "And it would have been rather churlish to refuse the chance of having a drink with you on your birthday, Sarah." He raised his glass slightly. "Happy birthday—and a happy year!" His smile barely reached his eyes.

The words reminded her—as they were meant to do—of her birthday a year ago which she had spent with him: he had toasted her then in the same words and it had been a promise that he would ensure her happiness during the year to come. It was bitter-sweet to remember the happiness they had known—happiness tinged with a vague uncertainty, a fear that her love would avail her nothing, a suspicion that David did not include marriage in his plans for the future. It was a cruel reminder—but David had proved that he could be cruel. Possibly the ruthless streak in his character had appealed to her for Sarah never stopped at anything to get her own way in life. Like had called to like—

and she had known from the first moment of meeting David Montrose that he was the only man who complemented her fully and in every way.

She smiled calmly. "Thank you, David." She turned to greet his companion—a man who had frequently accompanied them on social occasions, a friend of David's whom she had never liked but accepted for his sake. The dislike was mutual and recognised but they tolerated each other. In the latter months of her affair with David, Sarah had begun to suspect that Philip Russell influenced him strongly where marriage was concerned. Philip was a cynic: a disastrous marriage had given him a bitter outlook on life in general and women in particular; his cynical comments had definitely gone a long way in persuading David that love was ephemeral and only to be taken lightly and that marriage was the last resort of the lonely.

"We've just heard about your engagement," Philip said drily. "I should like to meet the man and offer him my condolences."

Sarah longed to slap his face but she

orced a laugh to her lips. "I expected a quip like that from you!" she told him lightly. She turned back to David. "I'm going to marry Andrew Whitaker. I think I must have mentioned his name to you from time to time, David."

"You did," he returned. "But I imagined he was rather senile—you always referred to him as an old friend of the family. I vaguely recall that you thought him a bore—but it would seem that you've changed your mind."

A faint flush stained her cheeks. "Andrew is far from senile, I assure you," she managed to retort.

"Perhaps he's wealthy," Philip inserted cynically. "Money can compensate for a great deal of boredom, I believe."

Sarah tightened her lips. David spoke to his friend. "Philip, old man—Sarah needs a drink. Would you fight your way to the bar? Peter doesn't seem to be doing very well—he lacks your air of authority."

Philip glanced from David to Sarah and a sardonic smile twisted his lips. Then he moved away and left them standing together.

For a moment, they were both silent.

Sarah twisted the ring on her finger, seeking frantically for words to ease the tension of the atmosphere, wishing desperately that he had not accompanied Peter Joslin that evening. It had been possible to cling to her determination to marry Andrew during the last week when she had stayed away from those places where she might perchance meet David: now her resolution was weakening because he stood by her side and she need only glance up to see his familiar face, the gleaming blond hair and the bright blue eyes, and clean-cut line of his jaw, the slender, straight nose and the humorous, mobile lips.

"Philip still succeeds in annoying you," he remarked at length.

She shrugged. "He's unimportant."

"You're looking very well—and very beautiful," he told her. She looked up and his eyes were warm now, smiling with the familiar, endearing intimacy which had always touched her heart. She sternly quelled the vibrant response of her being to the look in his eyes. "Are you happy too?"

"Certainly I am," she asserted firmly.

His smile was tinged with doubt. "I wonder."

"How are you, David?" she asked quickly, hating the need to make empty conversation but determined to steer clear of any discussion on her engagement to Andrew.

"I'm fine, thanks."

"I suppose you're very busy, as usual?" He was a successful barrister and he had the keen, legal mind and shrewd perception which she had always found difficult to deceive.

"I'm handling the Bowen case," he told her.

She nodded. "I read about it in one of the papers. I saw you with Caroline at the *Camino* last week—combining business with pleasure, I suspect?"

He smiled. "Why not? She's an attractive and intelligent young woman. Why didn't you join us for a drink?"

Her eyes flashed. "I decided against it —you were much too engrossed to be interested in old friends."

"It was an interesting conversation," he replied smoothly. "But you and Caroline are friends, aren't you?"

"We were," Sarah returned curtly.

He raised an eyebrow. "Past tense."

Swiftly she endeavoured to cover up the momentary revelation of jealousy. "She's been abroad, hasn't she? I haven't seen her for months. I must get in touch with her when I'm in Town again."

He produced a cigarette case and flicked it open with an adroit movement of his wrist. "Why not get in touch with me at the same time?" he suggested. "I'd be delighted to take you out to lunch—it would be almost like old times."

Her eyes narrowed. "Almost—but not quite, David. I don't think that's a very good idea."

He inclined his head to smile down at her, his eyes twinkling mischievously. "You of all people thinking of the conventions, Sarah!"

"I wasn't thinking of the conventions," she retorted. "I just don't think it's a good idea to meet you again—for lunch or anything else."

He shrugged. "Just as you like—but I think you're being silly, my dear. We used to have some good times together. I should very much like to meet you occasionally and talk over those times. Is there anything objectionable in such a suggestion? Do you really want to live the rest of your life without ever seeing me again —except by chance?"

Sarah was sorely tempted. How easy it would be to accept his invitation, to agree with his point of view, to meet him occasionally even if those meetings only meant partings and pain. But Andrew would never understand that she could meet David from time to time without any intention of disloyalty to him. Could she blame him? It would be an act of disloyalty no matter how she soothed her conscience —and she could gain nothing by meeting David as he suggested.

"Let's leave it at that, shall we?" David went on smoothly. "You know where to reach me—and I'll always be available to meet you if you change your mind. I think you'll get in touch with me, Sarah."

Philip returned at that moment with the drinks, Peter Joslin close behind him and Sarah was relieved of the necessity of making a reply. Conversation became general and after a few minutes, she excused herself from their company and went in search of Andrew.

Frances met her in the doorway of the drawing-room. Her eyes held a faint accusation. "Surely that was David Montrose?" she asked.

Sarah was startled. "How do you know?"

"I've seen enough photographs of him," Frances reminded her. "What on earth is he doing here tonight?"

"Peter Joslin brought him. Obviously his idea of a joke!"

Frances glanced at the three men. "Unless he thought it was possible to reconcile you with David—and it was his good deed for the day. He didn't know about your engagement, I suppose?"

"Peter? No, of course not. Have you seen Andrew?"

"He was talking to Simon just now. Running away from David, Sarah?" Frances asked shrewdly.

"What do you mean? Oh, there's Andrew. Excuse me, Frances." Sarah brushed past her cousin and hurried to the safety of Andrew's side.

Frances looked after her—and then

turned again to study David Montrose. He was more handsome than his photographs had portrayed. She could understand why Sarah had fallen so heavily for him—Sarah had always placed too much importance upon physical attractions. There was a faint air of arrogance about the man. So he was the man who had monopolised Sarah's thoughts and emotions for over a year— yet she had never brought him to Kendrick House and her family had never been given the opportunity to meet him. So he was the man that Frances had firmly believed Sarah meant to marry—yet she had announced her engagement to Andrew and for several weeks the name of David Montrose had not been heard on her lips.

David glanced in her direction—and then glanced again. Because she was studying him so blatantly, he smiled—a rich, intimate smile. Frances received the impression that he would smile in such a manner at any woman who caught his notice, however briefly. But there was something infectious in the curve of his lips—and she found to her surprise that her own lips curved in response. He detached himself from his friends and crossed towards her.

She said swiftly: "Aren't you David Montrose?"

"Yes, I am," he replied easily.

"I'm Frances Kendrick, Sarah's cousin," she told him.

His smooth brow wrinkled in a slight frown. "Have we ever met? Forgive me, but . . ."

She interrupted him hastily. "No, we haven't met, Mr. Montrose."

His smile held a faint question. "Yet you knew me?"

"I recognised you from photographs that Sarah has shown me occasionally," she explained.

"I see," he said quietly. He looked about him. "This is quite a festive occasion, isn't it?"

"Everyone seems to be enjoying themselves," Frances replied. She studied him covertly through her long lashes. "Sarah must have been pleased to see you tonight —she didn't expect you, I know."

He looked down at her. "She hid her pleasure remarkably well, Miss Kendrick. I'm sure she didn't bargain for my presence on the night that her engagement to another man was announced."

Inanely, Frances said: "Sarah didn't tell you about Andrew?"

"Not a word but that isn't very surprising. I haven't seen her for several weeks and I believe it was a snap decision —or am I mistaken?"

"I think most people expected Sarah to marry Andrew eventually," Frances replied slowly. She looked up into the fair, handsome features of David Montrose and she tried to look past the polite façade of his expression. What did he really feel? Was he really so unconcerned about Sarah's engagement as he seemed—or was he shocked and hurt by the unexpectedness of her decision? Had he ever responded at all to Sarah's love for him— or had he merely been amusing himself?

She tried to plumb the depths of this handsome man and discover what had attracted Sarah to him in the first place. Was it only his undeniable good looks, his easy charm and the air of arrogant sophistication which clung to him. Was he a man with a strong magnetic appeal for women? Or had Sarah sensed his hidden qualities

49

and determined to know him better and to win him for herself? There was no answer to the age-old question of why a particular type of man attracted a particular type of woman and vice versa. Frances was convinced that just as Andrew was the only man who could ignite the flame of love in her heart so David Montrose was the only man capable of stirring emotion within her cousin's being.

"So I gather," he returned quietly. He was intrigued by this girl who studied him so searchingly. "But you didn't?"

She hesitated briefly. Then she said: "A little while ago I believed that Sarah was practically engaged to you, Mr. Montrose." She only realised when the words were out how tactless they were.

His glance was sharp. "Did Sarah give you that impression?"

"Not exactly," she began and then she lifted her chin and amended her reply. "Frankly, yes, she did. I know she hoped to marry you—and I know that she was very happy with the prospect. Then suddenly she ceased to talk about you and I realised that something was wrong between you but it wasn't my business and I didn't ask questions."

"It still isn't your business," he said smoothly, so smoothly that he managed to sound courteous.

"I'm still not asking questions," she reminded him swiftly.

A crooked smile touched his lips. "I assure you that Sarah always knew that I had no intention of marrying her. To quote that much-used tag: we were just good friends—at least, from my point of view."

There was something about that smile which told her the truth. She read in his blue eyes something of the anguish and pain which contracted her own heart and she was both surprised and compassionate. David Montrose was in love with Sarah—she could sense it now and she felt like crying a denial of his words. They were not true! Or if they were, then he had only realised since his break with Sarah that he loved her—and he was too proud to let her or anyone else know the truth. Did you assert too often that you weren't the marrying kind? she silently asked of him. Did you make it too obvious that Sarah was wasting her time if she hoped to marry you? And is that the reason why you were unable to retract and admit how you really felt and ask her to marry you?

She was unconscious that her blue-grey eyes were raised to his face with an intensity of appeal which mingled oddly with compassion. David studied her small face. Sarah had spoken of her cousin in the same careless manner in which she referred to family and friends—and he had never felt any curiosity about the young woman. He had not expected to find her so attractive, so youthfully slender, so oddly appealing with her lovely eyes fringed by long, velvety lashes. Her sweet, musical voice was enchanting. He knew a faint stirring of interest—and in the far reaches of his mind an idea was born.

"I wonder why we haven't met before," he said and all his charm was to the fore.

Frances looked away swiftly, shyly. The sudden gleam of admiration in his eyes clashed violently with the new conviction that he was in love with Sarah. "I seldom go to Town," she replied.

"Then it's time you did," he countered with a smile. "Come up one day next week and let me take you to a show. No, I mean it," he went on, sensing that she was about to demur. "I should enjoy it very much."

Impulsively she nodded. "So should I, Mr. Montrose. Very well, I'll come."

"David," he amended gently. "Shall I telephone to confirm the arrangement?"

"If you would."

"Is there any particular show you'd like to see?" he wanted to know and for the next few minutes they discussed the current theatrical presentations—and while they talked, Frances wondered why she had so impulsively accepted his invitation. She did not know David Montrose except through Sarah's revelations of his character. But she felt strangely at ease with him and she knew that she would meet him and enjoy the evening in his company. They had one essential bond in common—a love for someone unattainable. It would be an odd situation if they became good friends but Frances did not pause to think of the consequences of such a friendship.

With the promise that he would telephone within a day or two, David returned to his friends—and Frances was again caught up in the business of attending to the smooth running of the evening. She was pleased when he came in search of her to bid her goodnight when he left with his friends. She noticed that he made no attempt to speak to Sarah again and that Sarah deliberately avoided David and his friends during the brief hour they remained at Kendrick House.

The party went on into the early hours but eventually the last guests took their leave. Frances was the last to go up to her room, tired yet content with the success of the evening.

Alone in her bedroom she undressed slowly. Then she sat down at her dressing-table, loosened the neat coil of her chestnut hair and began to brush it vigorously until it gleamed and shone in the subdued lighting. It fell past her shoulders in a burnished mass of vitality and colour, enriching her looks to soft beauty.

She hoped that David Montrose would telephone as he had promised. Andrew had been the centre of her dreams for so long now that she had seldom looked at another man—and now she realised how much of her life she had wasted. She was not hoping that romance lay in David's direction—that was unthinkable—but a vague idea stirred in her mind that he might be the means of fulfilling her dreams.

She could not help the conviction that Sarah had turned to Andrew only out of pique and a certainty that David would never marry her. If Frances was right, then Sarah would certainly resent any friendship that sprang up between her own cousin and the man she loved. If Frances were to emphasise that friendship, even out of all proportion, surely Sarah would realise that David was more important to her than Andrew and break her engagement. Andrew would be hurt—that was inevitable—but Frances would be both available and willing to ease his sense of loss and time must heal. She loved Andrew—and she knew that Sarah could never bring him happiness. She would go to any lengths to prevent their marriage and much as she hated deception, she would play a part with David Montrose's assistance until Sarah came to her senses! Surely David would be only too willing to agree to her plan once he realised that it might mean Sarah's freedom and renewed hope for his own love . . .

4

THE telephone shrilled its strident summons as Sarah came down the wide staircase, her hand trailing lightly on the polished balustrade. She nodded to the elderly slow-moving Travers. "It's all right—I'll answer it," she said, intercepting his unhurried progress across the hall. He retreated behind the green baize door which led to the staff quarters.

Sarah moved to the hall table and picked up the receiver. "Kendrick House," she announced clearly yet quietly. A familiar voice spoke in her ear and she was stunned for a moment: then her heart began to pound and her voice was breathless as she said: "David? Is that really you?"

"Sarah? I thought so," he replied smoothly. "How are you?"

She ignored his polite query. "I thought you asked for my cousin," she said lightly, laughing softly. "Distortion on the line, I suppose."

"But I did ask for your cousin," he responded quietly.

She was silent. Then she said slowly: "I see. Just a minute, David—I'll call her to the phone." She put the receiver down and looked at it unseeingly, making no move to go in search of her cousin. Why did David want to speak to Frances? What reason could he possibly have for telephoning her? Fervently she wished that she had allowed Travers to answer the summons so that she could have been spared the humiliation of jealousy which surged through her.

Slowly she crossed the hall to the drawing-room and opened the door. Frances was seated at a small bureau busy with the household accounts. She looked up as Sarah entered and smiled. "Looking for me?"

"Yes. A call for you, Frances." She looked with narrowed eyes at the girl in the soft tangerine sweater and grey skirt. "It's David Montrose."

The faintest trace of a flush stained Frances' cheeks. "Oh! Thank you, Sarah —I was expecting him to call me." She rose from her chair and walked towards the door, avoiding the searching gaze which Sarah directed at her. Quietly she closed the door of the drawing-room behind her and went to the telephone.

Sarah took a cigarette from a box which lay on a nearby table and with trembling hands ignited a silver table lighter. She resisted the temptation to listen to the one-sided conversation although she could hear the faint rise and fall of her cousin's voice in the hall. David must have met Frances here at Kendrick House when he came with Peter and Philip to the party. Had he found something to attract him in the demure face and figure of Frances? The pain and jealousy which fermented within her was almost unbearable.

She smoked her cigarette with swift, uneasy inhalations, pacing the room with angry movements. Her brain seethed with questions to which she had no answers. Why should David telephone Frances? And why had Frances blushed at the sound of his name? Was it true that she had been expecting the call from David? Had they known each other before the night of the party unknown to her?

The door opened and she spun round

swiftly but it was not Frances who entered. Andrew greeted her with a warm smile and crossed the room to brush her cheek with a gentle kiss.

"Have I kept you waiting?" he asked. "I had some trouble with the car."

She had completely forgotten that they had arranged to go for a drive. She looked at him with the eyes of a stranger and then she pulled herself together as a tiny frown creased his brow.

"I didn't realise you were late," she told him and turned away to stub her cigarette. "Is the car all right now?"

"Yes—it was only a minor fault and I managed to put it right. We're not likely to break down on the way to the coast . . ." He caught her arm and turned her towards him. "Is anything wrong? Are you quite well?"

She forced a laugh to her lips. "I'm fine!"

"Sure? You look a little pale and you're not really listening to me," he told her.

She smiled up at him. "Sorry, Andrew. I was thinking of something else. I'm quite well, I assure you. Would you like coffee before we leave or shall we stop on the road?"

He accepted her explanation at its face value but his spirits sank a little. He knew that something troubled her and he wondered if she were regretting her promise to marry him. Throughout the years they had been friends, she had confided in him easily, spoken naturally and without reserve of any problem which worried her, great or small. But since their engagement, he had sensed a slight reticence on her part, a reluctance to speak the complete truth to him, and there were times when he was certain that she pretended to a contentment and lightness of heart to conceal her innermost feelings.

He was in no position to dispute her claims of present happiness and excited expectation of the future as his wife but he could not deny the doubts he knew as to the wisdom of the step they planned.

Deciding to stop for coffee en route to the coast, they left the house, passing Frances who was still talking to David Montrose on the telephone. She waved a hand as they crossed the hall but did not break off her conversation. She laughed softly in reply to something that David said to her and Sarah's hand tightened convulsively on Andrew's arm. He looked down at her swiftly but something in her expression forestalled the comment he was about to make.

Andrew drove swiftly but capably along the country lanes. Sarah was silent by his side, her face averted so that he might not guess at her thoughts from the expression in her eyes. The scenery sped by unnoticed and unappreciated. Andrew flicked on the radio and the strains of music invaded the car.

"How soon do you want to stop for coffee?" he asked.

"Whenever you like," she replied indifferently.

He glanced at her briefly and then turned his gaze back to the long ribbon of road. His strong brown hands were steady on the wheel.

The hum of the tyres linked with the sound of David's name which kept repeating itself in Sarah's brain. Her heart was heavy and she bit her lip against the tumult of misery which filled her being. Where had she failed him that he had not wanted to marry her? She had been so sure of the love which he never admitted, so sure that her patience and understanding would eventually know its own reward, so sure that one day he would realise how much he needed her as his wife. But slowly the truth had dawned on her that he did not love or need her, that he would never marry her, that she was throwing away the precious months of her youth on a man who sought her company only through motives of affection and friendship.

She remembered their last evening together—and wished that the memory was not so vivid still. Dining at a famous London restaurant, her happiness in his company tinged with sadness at his continued default and a bitter resolve to know the truth from his own lips, she had forced him to admit that he would not marry her either now or one day in the future. His blue eyes had smiled yet they had held a hint of regret that he must cause her pain. His voice had been light and confident yet she knew that he disliked facing the issue and would prefer to carry on the association indefinitely.

The echo of her sharp refusal to do so and her determined claim that she had no intention of meeting him again still rang in her ears. He had shrugged, smiled and agreed that they should part. It had been Sarah's turn to regret—regret the ultimatum she had thrown at him, regret her hasty determination to know once and for all whether he meant to marry her or not— but she could not regret the many months of happiness she had known with him or the joy she had found in loving him even if both happiness and joy had been touched with humiliation and disappointment.

She could find excuses for him: he was ambitious and believed that a man moved faster through life on his own; he was afraid of the responsibilities and bonds of marriage; he had been too much influenced by the detestable Philip Russell throughout the years; it was not his fault if he was unable to love her and she must be grateful for the affection and tender consideration and kindness he had shown to her. So many excuses. But they did not help to heal the pain in her heart nor did they soothe the ache of missing him so much. He was constantly in her thoughts.

Now, guided by an impulse, she had embarked on a lifelong deception of Andrew who must never know that she still loved and wanted David with all her heart. No doubt there would be many occasions when Andrew would find her cold and unresponsive, impatient with his gentle demands and unappreciative of his good qualities—occasions when David would dominate her thoughts and emotions to the exclusion of everyone and everything else. But she had given her word and she would not go back on it. She must fight down the need for David and concentrate on making Andrew happy and content in their marriage.

Suddenly she was beseiged by the desperate longing for the security of Andrew's name which had driven her to suggest that they should be married. Andrew would look after her. He would protect her from further pain and unhappiness. Life with him might be dull and uneventful and lacking the ecstacy which she could have known with David—but she needed to be surrounded with the shield of dulled emotions. When David was the be-all and end-all of her existence, her emotions had been hurled and tossed about on the sea of love to such an extent that she had felt bruised and surfeited and breathless, longing for a respite from the heights and depths of her love for him. Life with Andrew as her husband would bring peace and calm after the tumult—and she desperately needed a breathing space during which her emotions could lay dormant and untouched.

She forgot that she would probably tire very quickly of such a breathing space. She forgot that Andrew's emotions were entitled to consideration. She did not pause to consider that looking upon marriage to Andrew as a refuge and a harbour could scarcely promise much happiness for either of them after the first few months. She did not consider the possibility that she might be making the biggest mistake of her life, that one could not snatch at marriage in the hope that it would bring relieving balm to a bruised heart and injured pride.

She turned abruptly towards the man by her side. "Andrew—must we wait six months?"

He was startled by the unexpectedness

of the question—then he reminded himself that he had known she would return to the attack sooner or later. They had discussed their wedding date on the morning after the party and he had been firm in his resolution to give her six months to be really sure of her decision. She had consented with scarcely any argument—but he could not know that then she had been clinging to a new hope that David might miss her after all and had attended her party with the intention of seeing her again, that her own resolution had weakened overnight, that she had been prepared to delay her wedding to Andrew indefinitely in case David wanted her back again. Neither could he know that now she was filled with despairing certainty that David had forgotten the happiness they had shared and was prepared—even willing—to seek the company of other women, that she had no future unless it was as Andrew's wife.

"I thought we had settled the point," he said slowly, giving himself time to consider the implication of her words. She was suspiciously eager to marry him and he wished he knew her real motives. Did she plan to show David Montrose that he was not the only man in the world? Did she hope to hurt the man through him? Did she still love Montrose but, knowing he was beyond her reach, resigned herself to another man's arms—no matter who the man!—simply because she was filled with a need to be married, to have a home and a husband and family of her own? Was it just a passing phase or did she really believe that her happiness lay in a future with him?

He had believed that he knew Sarah intimately. Now he realised that he scarcely knew her at all, that he could not hazard a guess at the workings of her mind, that he was a stranger to the emotions within her. It was not enough that he loved her. It was not enough that he had known her since she was in her early teens, had watched her grow into a lovely girl and then a beautiful woman, had played the part of confidant when she needed to talk of her private thoughts and feelings. She had promised to marry him —and he felt that he was engaged to a woman he did not know or understand. Could they possibly be happy together?

"There's nothing to wait for," she told

him swiftly, sincerely. "I want to marry you now. Why are you so hesitant, Andrew? Have you changed your mind about me? Did I force you into an engagement that you can't welcome or want?"

He took a hand from the steering-wheel and found her fingers, squeezing them reassuringly. "I want to marry you, Sarah. But only if you're really sure that you can be happy with me." He turned his head to smile at her. "I love you too much to allow you to make a mistake. If you have any doubts, tell me now. I won't bear malice and we shall still be friends."

Petulantly she moved her hand away from his touch. "I haven't any doubts. Oh, I'm tired of all this discussion. I had no idea that getting you to marry me would be so difficult! You seem to think that you're dealing with a child, Andrew. I'm an adult woman and I know what I'm doing."

He was silent for a long moment. Then he said slowly, unemotionally: "Very well, Sarah. When do you want to be married?"

"As soon as possible!" she told him emphatically.

He nodded. "Shall I arrange for a

special licence? Then we can be married at any time. How long would you need to make the necessary arrangements—a week? A fortnight?"

She caught her breath. He had fallen in with her wishes—and contrarily she wished that she had not once more forced the issue. She could not retract now and she damned her impulsive nature. Then she told herself that the sooner she was Andrew's wife, the sooner she would feel secure . . . She would be forced to accept the new way of life and forced to drive the memory of David from her heart and mind.

He heard the faint sound of sharply-indrawn breath and wondered at the thoughts which must be racing through her mind. He felt a brief compassion for the turmoil of her emotions. Poor Sarah! Did she really know what she wanted? Would he be doing the right thing to aid and abet her in following up the strange impulse which had moved her to marry him? She might seem a stranger to him during these difficult days but she was still the charming, warm-hearted and loveable Sarah that he had always known and loved and wanted for his own. He felt a new confidence steal through his veins. He could make her happy. He could promise contentment and security and they had an excellent foundation for marriage. He recalled that Frances had pointed the latter out to him and he approved her shrewd perception. Frances knew them both well and she had not attempted to dissuade either of them from taking the step they proposed to take. Surely it was the wisest decision Sarah had ever made in her life? They would not need to get to know each other. They would not expect too much from each other or from marriage itself. He would not be disappointed in her qualities because he knew her so well. They would not be bewildered and hurt when the first raptures of marriage settled down into quiet contentment because they did not expect joyous ecstasy or wild heights of passion. He loved her as he had always loved her—a quiet, undemanding and unselfish love. In time perhaps she would learn to love him in the same way —and he would be content. If all he ever knew was her constant affection and loyalty and the sweet warmth of her personality—he would still be content in the knowledge that she was his wife.

He did not prompt her to answer him and within a few moments she began to speak of arrangements and the date was fixed.

It seemed strange to be talking of her wedding to Andrew while another man had the power to melt her resolve with one glance, to spirit her heart to soaring heights with the sound of his voice, to fill her entire being with love and tenderness when she thought of him. But she would never marry David and the only way she could live without him and know peace of mind was to become Andrew's wife and live with him in quiet contentment.

Soon they stopped at a small restaurant for coffee and final details were settled over a cigarette and the fragrant beverage. Some of the constraint had left them both and they were more at ease with each other.

Sarah smiled across the table at Andrew and felt a surge of affection for him. Dear Andrew—dear, good and reliable Andrew. He was the only man she could possibly marry, the only man who would never fail her, would always understand her and would make her his first consideration. She must never let him suspect that he was only second-best and perhaps time would prove that second-best was in fact the best. She was adult enough to accept the inevitable even though there might be occasions when she railed against the unkind fate which had denied her David's love and the joy she could have known with him. It was futile to long for David—she must do all in her power to suppress the treacherous memories and to erase the past. The future was all-important—her future with Andrew and because he loved her she must strive to make him happy and try to respond to his love. Surely it would not be so difficult. She had always been fond of him: they were excellent friends; they had many things in common and she believed that he would do his best to make allowances for her. At least she had not pretended to a love she did not feel—and she knew that this she could never do. One day she might be able to love him—in an entirely different way in which she loved David but sufficient to make her life with Andrew not only tolerable but enjoyable.

As though he read her mind, he leaned

forward and took her hand, searching her eyes. "Sarah, there's only one thing I want you to remember." She met his gaze levelly, warmly. "I love you very much and my one hope is that one day you'll love me in return—if only a little. All I ask is that you never try to deceive me. Don't pretend to anything you don't feel —not now or ever. I shall know the truth for myself no matter how well you play a part. I'm still not sure why you want to marry me but I know that I want you as my wife and I'm prepared to take any risks. If you're unhappy with me and want your freedom at any time don't be afraid to tell me so. I won't be possessive. My only concern is your happiness."

Tears sprang to her eyes. His words were so typical of his generous nature and the unselfishness of the love he knew for her. Briefly she felt that she must not make use of him as a safe harbour—then she realised that a few months or years of happiness with her as his wife would content him as long as she was content and she determined to make a success of her marriage at no matter what cost to herself and her own futile dreams.

5

DAVID produced his cigarettes and offered them to Frances. She accepted a cigarette and smiled her thanks, a little shyly. She had been at ease with him on the telephone but now, seated beside him in the cocktail bar where they had arranged to meet, she felt a little at a loss for words. He flicked his lighter into life and she bent over the flame, resting her hand briefly on his wrist to steady the lighter.

She watched him as he lighted his own cigarette. She wondered if he knew that Sarah planned to marry Andrew in ten days' time. She shrank from breaking the news to him and hoped that he would have seen the announcement for himself in the Press. She did not want to talk about Sarah and Andrew. It had been too painful to discover that Sarah really intended and apparently wanted to marry Andrew. She had been forced to the conclusion that Sarah had mistaken her feelings for David

Montrose and had always loved Andrew—and it was a bitter blow to Frances to realise that her own deep love for Andrew had no future.

David was aware of her gaze. He was faintly puzzled by this young woman. Her demure appeal could not be compared in any way with Sarah's vital effect on his emotions yet she held a strange attraction for him. Perhaps it was the contrast between the two women. Perhaps he hoped to find some resemblance to Sarah in her cousin. Or else he unconsciously sought consolation with a woman as far removed as possible from the memory of Sarah. There had to be some explanation why he had followed up the tentative suggestion that they should meet again—and it was not solely the vaguely-formulated plan of proving to Sarah that she was not the only woman in the world.

He recalled the announcement he had read of her pending marriage to Andrew Whitaker. He had been stunned and incredulous at first—then slowly realisation of the truth had dawned upon him. He had been wrong to believe that Sarah was hoping to stir him to action, to bring him running back to her arms and that her engagement was nothing but pretence on her part. He had resolved that he would not be driven into a corner by her wiles. A proud, self-sufficient and supremely confident man, he was prepared to wait until she realised that he meant to take no steps to prevent her proposed marriage, convinced that she would break her engagement eventually on some pretext or other, secure in the knowledge that she would find it impossible to forget her love for him.

Now he realised how foolish he had been. He had taken Sarah's love for granted all those months, unwilling to commit himself irrevocably until he was really sure of his feelings and their lasting power. He had not blamed Sarah for losing patience with him. He had not blamed her for lacking faith in his intentions. He had been willing when she suggested that their association should come to an end, confident that the break would last only a few brief months and would give him time to assess his emotions, knowing that she meant more to him than any other woman ever had before or was likely to mean in the future but still not ready to accept the bonds and responsibilities of marriage.

Sarah had walked out of his life—and into the arms of another man and now it seemed that Andrew Whitaker had provided a happiness that he had failed to bring Sarah. He had to admit to himself that Sarah must love Whitaker: she was not a child and she understood the seriousness of her decision to marry the man; she had never treated the subject of marriage lightly. Whether she had fallen in love on the rebound or whether she had always loved Whitaker and mistaken her emotions, David did not know—and now it did not seem to matter very much. All that mattered was that he had lost Sarah —and the sense of loss filled his entire being. But the fault lay at his own door. He had thrown away his chance of happiness.

He drew deeply on his cigarette and looked about him. The cocktail bar was an attractive place with its subtle lighting, the reflected gleam of bottles and highly-polished glasses, the long bar with its drawn-up stools and the many softly-tinted mirrors which decorated the walls. Odd that he should have chosen to meet Frances Kendrick here—this had been one of Sarah's favourite bars and they had frequently met to drink cocktails, to clasp hands and to enjoy each other's company in the warmly-intimate atmosphere of the place.

Frances found it somewhat disconcerting that her reflection should be repeated again and again in the wall mirrors but at the same time it was reassuring. She could not resist the occasional glance to ensure that her hair was smooth and her make-up intact. She caught David's eyes as she turned away from a swift glance—and he smiled almost indulgently.

"You're looking fine," he assured her.

She laughed softly. "I suppose it's the inherent vanity in us all that makes a mirror so irresistible."

He waved a hand airily. "Look around —not many can resist the occasional peep at themselves. Some are openly studying the effect of a facial expression or a carefully nonchalant gesture of the hand. I find it rather amusing." He turned to her abruptly. "You haven't been here before?"

Frances shook her head. "No. I very seldom come to Town," she reminded him.

"Surely life is rather dull for you in the country?"

"I don't think so. Perhaps I'm not cut out for the gay social whirl." Her smile was half-apologetic. "I enjoy the occasional visit to Town," she went on. "But I find plenty to do at home."

He toyed with his glass. "You're very different to Sarah. She used to complain of feeling stifled in the country. Yet she's marrying a man who feels as you do about the gay social whirl—she used to speak of Andrew Whitaker as a stick in the mud who preferred his home, his books and music, and the country life to anything else. I can't imagine her settling down very easily."

Frances met his eyes levelly. "You've seen the announcement?"

"That a marriage has been arranged and will take place? Yes, I did. Next Friday, isn't it? Sarah isn't wasting any time but she was always the impetuous type." He indicated her glass. "Finish your drink.

We've just time for one more before we leave for the theatre."

Obediently she finished the contents of her glass. He turned away to catch the eye of the bar-tender. It pleased her that he found no difficulty in doing so. She thought of him as the type of man who would procure a taxi while others vainly hailed the apparently-blind drivers, who would be assured of a good table in a restaurant or nightclub while others had to be content with the obscure positions. Was it merely his air of personal magnetism, the superficial attraction of his undeniable good looks and easy charm, the touch of arrogant authority in his bearing? It was easy to understand why Sarah had fallen in love with him—or else believed herself to be in love with him.

When the fresh drinks were brought, he picked up his glass. "Should we drink to Sarah's happiness?" he suggested, half-mockingly.

Frances looked at him keenly, her head inclined a little to one side. "You don't believe that she will be happy, do you?"

"Frankly?" He shrugged. "It's very difficult to give an opinion. I don't know the man she's marrying. I don't know how Sarah feels about it herself. I could say that it's all happened too suddenly—but one must remember that she has known Whitaker for years and presumably she's confident of finding happiness with him. I hope she will be happy," he added quietly and the words were sincere.

"How can you sit back while Sarah marries someone else?" she asked urgently. The words escaped her almost of their own volition and she regretted them immediately as his eyes froze to ice.

He was silent, studying her, considering her question, startled by the unexpected realisation that she was aware of his feelings for Sarah—and wondering that one woman could be so perceptive where another had been so blind.

"What makes you think I'd do anything else?" he asked after a long pause.

She hesitated. Could she be wrong? Had she misconstrued the expression in his eyes on the night of Sarah's party? "I think you're in love with Sarah," she said eventually.

He raised an eyebrow. "I see." He did not try to deny the truth of her statement.

"Do you think that gives me the right to interfere in her affairs? Do you think she would appreciate it if I tried to make her change her mind?"

She toyed absently with the stem of her glass. "I don't know. I thought she loved you—and that she'd decided to marry Andrew because . . ." She broke off.

"Because I'd made it clear that I didn't mean to marry her?" he finished for her.

"Yes. Too clear, possibly. I think you regret it now," she said quietly.

He shrugged. "It's a little late for regrets. I wasted my opportunities. I can't blame Sarah. I thought she loved me but her plans to marry Whitaker as soon as she possibly can prove otherwise."

"I'm afraid so," she admitted and her voice held a note of sadness.

He glanced at her with narrowed eyes. "Why are you so interested in your cousin's marriage to Andrew Whitaker?" She looked at him and then glanced away quickly but not before his keen perception read the truth in her eyes. "I see. Because you hoped to marry him yourself." He added gently: "I'm sorry."

She laughed: a brittle little sound that

held no humour. "Oh, I had no foundation for my hopes. Andrew has never been interested in me. His world has always revolved around Sarah." Her voice was slightly bitter.

His blue eyes were almost tender. "It isn't the end of the world, you know, Frances," he said gently. "There are other men—and other women."

"Not for me," she replied and meant it with all her heart.

"Then you wouldn't agree to any suggestion on my part that we should console each other?" he asked lightly.

"What do you mean?" she countered swiftly.

He touched her fingers with his hand. "I like you, Frances. I like your company. I admire your direct approach. I should like you to meet me again. I think we could be friends. I'm not suggesting anything else. But we're both in the same boat and it's essential that you should learn to forget Andrew Whitaker. I intend to forget Sarah. One cannot live indefinitely in the past, after all."

"You don't love Sarah very much!" she accused.

His eyes darkened. "On the contrary—I love her very deeply but next week she will be marrying another man. One has to start again—erase the past and find a new love. If you hanker for Andrew Whitaker, my dear, you're going to be a very unhappy woman and a very bitter one. So be sensible and make up your mind to find another man who can make you happy."

Frances could not deny that there was a certain amount of common-sense in his words. She had always known how Andrew felt about Sarah. There had never been any reason for her to believe that one day he might turn to her, even if Sarah had married someone else. She loved him but he was going to marry Sarah and it would be foolish to waste any more of her life in futile dreams of Andrew. She would have to look for the qualities she admired in another man. David Montrose was not a man who could inspire love in her heart but she found him attractive and she had no reason to reject his offer of friendship. She was certain to meet other men through him and perhaps one of them would have the power to take Andrew's place or at least to bring her a measure of happiness.

"I suppose that's all one can do," she said slowly.

His smile was approving. "It's not going to be easy for you, Frances. I do understand that. You'll be living very close to them and you can't avoid seeing them together. Whereas it's unlikely that Sarah and I will meet very often for we'll no longer move in the same circles. But you can rely on me to look after you whenever you choose to come to Town—and I hope you'll do so very often. You're much too young to stagnate in the country."

It was true that Frances felt stimulated by this trip to London. She had travelled up by an early train and enjoyed an afternoon of shopping. She had met an old school-friend in Regent Street by accident and it had been pleasant to have tea with her, to reminisce and to catch up on the news of their mutual friends, to talk of fashions and films and shows. Perhaps David was right when he spoke of stagnation. Perhaps her life was a little dull but while Andrew had been so frequently at Kendrick House and in the vicinity, she had been content. But his marriage to Sarah would bring about a great many changes and it was going to be painful for her to see them together and witness their happiness in each other. She did not consider leaving her home but it might be a good plan to spend more time in Town, to widen her interests and her circle of acquaintances, to get in touch again with old friends.

She wondered briefly why David Montrose should interest himself in her enough to offer friendship and the promise of his company whenever she was in London. Did he hope to have frequent news of Sarah through her? Or did he simply mean to ensure that she forgot Andrew all the sooner by providing her with a fuller social life?

As though he considered the matter closed, David finished his drink and threw her a glance of enquiry. She gathered up her bag and gloves and rose to her feet and they left the cocktail bar together.

The musical show was excellent and Frances was absorbed in the colour and spectacle, witty dialogue and lyrics and the splendid singing to such an extent that she was able to push all thoughts of Andrew and Sarah to the back of her mind. She was barely conscious of the man by her side. David was faintly bored but he found his enjoyment in watching the play of expression across his companion's face, her eager attentiveness, her evident delight in the entertainment. She seemed content in his company but he was left with the vague impression that she remained singularly untouched by his charm or personality—and this was a new thing for David Montrose who had been spoiled all his adult life where women were concerned. Perhaps Sarah's obvious warmth of feeling and eagerness to marry him had made him contrarily reluctant to admit his love and to commit himself: he had always found it too easy to win affection and admiration; the cool, remote type of woman stirred his interest more swiftly—and Sarah had been just that little too warmly impulsive. Frances Kendrick had not been eager to accept his offer of friendship. There still remained some doubt whether or not she would meet him again—and because he fancied that she would not, he was determined that she should. The need to conquer her reluctance was strong within him. Yet he hoped she would not be easily

won for he enjoyed the spirit of a chase—
he was a man and man was destined to be
the hunter. He soon tired of any woman
who made her interest in him too obvious.
Sarah had possessed the power to win his
love—and he knew that he loved her very
deeply, as he had assured her cousin. But
it was possible that he had failed to
recognise his love when Sarah was within
his reach because of the strange quirk of
his nature which preferred a reluctant
quarry rather than one who came more
than half-way to meet him.

As they left the theatre, merging with
the crowd who chattered gaily about the
show, David suggested a visit to a night-
club.

Frances glanced at the neat wrist-watch
she wore. "I don't think so," she said
thoughtfully. "I hoped to catch the eleven-
thirty train."

He smiled down at her. "Surely you
don't think I would let you travel by train
at night—on your own?" He took her
elbow and guided her through the mass of
people and they began to walk along the
pavements towards the side turning where
the car was parked. It was a damp, mild

night and slight rain was falling. "It won't take us very long to get to Avering by car, you know."

She demurred swiftly. "It's much too far, David, you'll be so late getting back."

"Supposing you let me worry about that?" he suggested easily.

"I should have made arrangements to stay overnight," she said slowly, "but it never occurred to me to do so."

"Next time—then our evening together needn't be so short," he told her.

She glanced up at him swiftly. "You're very confident that there will be a next time, aren't you?"

He opened the car door for her and she stepped in. Then he walked around the car to the driving side and joined her. He turned in his seat to smile at her. "Do you want to drive to Avering now—or shall we find a quiet pub for a last drink?"

"Oh, Avering!" she exclaimed. "If you insist on driving me home."

He turned on the ignition. "I do insist. I don't see the point in putting you on to a train when I have a perfectly good car at my disposal—in any case, it's scarcely the correct way to end an enjoyable evening."

He touched her hand briefly with his fingers before he released the brake. "You have enjoyed it, haven't you?"

"Very much," she assured him sincerely.

"So have I," he told her quietly.

Once they had left the busy thoroughfares of the city, the roads were comparatively empty and the car ate up the miles with ease. He switched on the radio and soft music accompanied the journey. As he had promised, it did not take very long to reach the small village and almost before Frances realised it, they were turning into the gates which guarded the long drive up to the house. They had exchanged few remarks during the journey. She had been content to listen to the radio and relax by his side, aware that he was a capable and competent driver, intrigued by the gaunt majesty of the countryside at night which was thrown into sudden relief by the car headlights and then once again plunged into darkness to merge with the velvet inkiness of the sky.

He stopped the car outside the house. Apart from a light which blazed from an upstairs window, the house was in darkness and silent in the stillness of the night.

David turned slightly in his seat and slid an arm along the back of France's seat so that he almost touched her shoulders. She tensed—and he sensed the stirring of her instincts. A slow smile curved her lips. His only intention had been to make his position comfortable—yet, like all women, she immediately imagined that he sought some payment for the evening's entertainment. He wondered how she would react if he drew her into his arms and sought the sweetness of her lips. Would she be willing and responsive—or would she be coldly angry and repulse him without hesitation? For a brief moment he toyed with the idea—and then he realised that she was completely unaware of him or the presence of his arm.

She was gazing at that lighted window —and he followed her gaze.

Sarah drew back abruptly and allowed the drapes to fall into place—but not before David had seen and recognised the auburn beauty of her hair and the slenderness of her lovely body wrapped in the flimsy negligée. She knew his car too well not to know that it was standing outside her house—and it needed no deduction on her part to know that her cousin had arrived home in his car.

"Sarah?" he asked softly but he knew the answer.

Frances nodded. "She must have heard the car." She pulled her coat about her. "Thank you for bringing me home, David—and thank you for a lovely evening."

He touched her cheek briefly with his fingers. "It was my pleasure," he told her. "May I telephone you again, Frances?"

She smiled at him—but it was an absent smile for her thoughts were with Sarah and that swift withdrawal from the window. "Of course. I shall look forward to hearing from you."

He moved swiftly and left the car. He opened the car door for her and gave her his hand as she stepped out, steadying her. His clasp firm, he drew her slightly towards him and brushed her cheek with his lips. "Goodnight, my dear."

She was startled by the unexpected caress and also by its odd tenderness. "Goodnight, David—and thank you again."

He watched as she hurried up the wide stone steps, fumbling in her bag for the doorkey. She turned to wave to him before she entered the house—and then she closed the door with an air of finality. David brought out his cigarette case and flicked it open. He stood for a few moments, smoking, looking up at that lighted window, half of his mind on the journey back to London and the other half on Sarah—and he wondered what she thought of his apparent interest in her cousin . . .

6

SARAH listened to the soft fall of her cousin's footsteps, noticed the faint hesitation outside her bedroom door and clenched her hands against the fear that Frances would knock lightly and enter. Had she moved too slowly from the window? Had both Frances and David been aware of her scrutiny and then the instinctive withdrawal? She had not meant to spy on them but the sound of the car had drawn her to the window, her curiosity stirred. She had been shocked, almost disbelieving, as she recognised David's car—then she remembered his telephone call to Frances and swiftly realised that her cousin must have gone up to Town to meet him.

A few moments later, she heard the gentle click as Frances closed the door of her own bedroom—and slowly the tension seeped from her still, slim body. She sank down on the edge of her bed and stared unseeingly across the room, her mind echoing David's name and her love for him conjuring memories of the unforgettable moments she had shared with him. How could she give him up so easily? How could she possibly marry Andrew while the tumult of love pounded in her veins and turned her limbs to water? How could she deny the longing for David which possessed her so strongly?

Then bitter remembrance caused her heart to twist with pain. She had not given David up without a struggle. She had fought against her pride, humbled herself in so many ways, in order to win his love and the promise of marriage—but he had slowly and inexorably forced her to the position where she had issued an ultimatum—and she had lost. It had never been his intention to marry her. He had known that she was not the woman who could stir love in his being but he had been content to let things drift indefinitely until he had tired of her subtle insistence that they should be married. Their association had not been the painful, unsatisfactory and frustrating affair for him as it had been for her—his heart had not been involved and he had lacked the perception and the understanding to know that every moment spent with him had been both a joy and a torment for her.

Her love for him had always been futile and it would remain so even if she did not marry Andrew. The future stretched bleak and empty before her no matter what path she chose to follow because David would not be waiting at the end of any one of them. With Andrew's love and understanding, his gentle consideration and kindness, she could find a measure of contentment—and perhaps in time she would be able to think of David and remember their affair without pain and bitterness. But she would always love him. Love came only once—the love she knew for David.

Again she wondered what attraction Frances held for him—why he should go out of his way to see her cousin again. Frances was such a simple, straightforward person, lacking the sophistication, the intriguing qualities, the looks and personality which David sought in a woman. Yet in some way she had managed to interest him.

The two cousins had always been close

friends and a strong bond of affection linked them yet Sarah could not help the shaft of jealousy which seized her in a grip so powerful that for a few moments she could feel nothing but hatred and animosity for Frances.

She closed her eyes against the force of emotion, her finger-nails digging sharply into the palms of her hands, her body rigid and arched with pain. Then, as swiftly as it rose in her, the feeling receded—and she was drained and empty. She stood up and slipped out of her flimsy negligée, kicked off her mules and eased her body between the cool sheets of the bed. She stretched out a hand to switch off the light and lay on her back in the darkness, trying to empty her mind of the whirling kaleidoscopic thoughts so that she could know some ease in sleep.

At last, she slept fitfully, her dreams haunted by David and Frances and Andrew. One dream, in which Frances sailed happily up the aisle with a husband on each arm—David and Andrew—leaving Sarah sobbing bitterly in the vestry, knowing that she had lost everything she loved to her cousin and was doomed to marry the cynical Philip Russell whom she hated, was so vivid that she woke to the sunlight streaming through the window with tears wet on her lashes and cheeks and her body still shuddering with emotion. She lay for a few moments, dazed, not quite sure whether it had all been a dream or not . . .

The next few days took on a dream-like quality for Sarah. Involved in wedding preparations, her marriage to Andrew came steadily nearer—yet she could not believe that she would really be his wife, really promise to love, honour and obey him, really leave her home and family to live with him for the rest of her life. If it had been David, how eagerly, how joyfully she would have anticipated all these things, how slowly the days would pass for her. But she was going to marry Andrew —and each morning as she realised that she was one day nearer that irrevocable step she knew a momentary panic, a mad impulse to take her car and drive away from Kendrick House and Avering and Andrew, heading for some unknown destination where she could remain until all the rumour and speculation and indignation had blown over. But each morning she knew that she would not run away. She had chosen her destiny with open eyes and a cold, clear-cut realisation of what marriage to Andrew entailed.

It was foolish to be afraid of life with Andrew when she knew him so well and trusted him implicitly—but she was afraid. She had never known him in any other rôle but that of a friend: he might prove to be entirely different as a husband with whom she would share all the intimacies of married life. She knew an incomprehensible panic when she tried to review all the things she knew about him. It was not enough to lump together his patience, his kindness and consideration, his loyal affection, his unfailing courtesy towards her, the interests they had in common, the similarity of their backgrounds. She had always taken him for granted but she had never realised it until now. Perhaps he would not always be so patient with her moods when she was his wife. Perhaps there would be occasions when his kindness and consideration would be less in evidence if she stirred him to anger. She realised that she had never seen Andrew out of temper but he was as human as any man and it was logical to suppose that he could feel anger and impatience. She could rely on his loyalty and affection—but would it prove to be enough when she had so little to give him in return. She would be loyal to him, she determined, and she could give him the same depth and warmth of affection he had always received from her—but would either of these things withstand years of marital experiences? She found it difficult to visualise a time when Andrew would fail to be courteous to her but marriage was such a close relationship and she would know him all moods. She must expect the day to dawn when he would be irritable or preoccupied or unwell and reveal primitive emotion in an unguarded moment.

She emphasised the importance of their mutual interests and similar background, reminding herself that he was one man who had yet to bore her with his personality. David was another whose company had never failed to stimulate her—but she must not allow her thoughts to dwell on David. She told herself that her chance of happiness with Andrew depended very much on their enjoyment of each other's company. They had always been able to converse for hours on many and varied subjects. They shared mutual tastes in music, literature, art and the theatre. They were both keen riders, swimmers and tennis-players. They had many mutual friends and much of their time would be taken up with entertaining and being entertained. She firmly rejected the reminder that Andrew disliked the emptiness of the social round, assuring herself that he would gladly escort her to the gay, lively functions which she enjoyed so much if only because he wanted to please her. She knew that she needed and would continue to need frequent visits to London, to the theatre, to parties and to the many social occasions which had always been a part of her life. Andrew had always preferred the country life but there would have to be adaptation on both sides to a new way of life in future.

Frances made no mention of her visit to London and Sarah determined not to raise the subject. She was a little surprised that Frances should be so secretive—and then wondered at her astonishment for her cousin had always been reticent about her affairs and her feelings. There was no reason why Frances should mention David or her appointment with him and Sarah decided that she was being tactful. She tried not to think of David and his apparent interest in Frances: she tried to repress the jealousy which burned in her as she studied her cousin with thoughtful eyes and endeavoured to determine the qualities which must have attracted David; above all, she tried to impress upon Andrew that she had no doubts about her promise to marry him.

He was not deceived. He sensed the resignation in her attitude and he was hurt but he was a man who had trained himself to conceal his feelings well and he gave no sign of the pain he knew that Sarah could not anticipate their wedding with joy or pleasure. He could not doubt that she meant to marry him but her real motives were completely unknown to him. He could only hope that she would find such happiness in their marriage that she never knew regret or sought to end it.

On the eve of the wedding, he gave her one last opportunity to change her mind.

He was a fair man and, much as he loved her, he was fully prepared to forgo his own happiness if necessary.

She was unpacking a wedding present which had arrived and he watched her neat, deft movements. He still found it hard to believe that within twenty-four hours she would be his wife. The very thought gave him a feeling of mingled pain and pleasure. How different everything would seem if she only loved him. As it was, their wedding plans had been imbued with a certain clinical coldness and method which he disliked intensely.

As she revealed the gift, she wrinkled her nose with distaste and turned to display it to him, half-laughing. "Why do so many people send things which they wouldn't give house room? Isn't this atrocious, Andrew? Oh well, it can be packed away with the other monstrosities."

He grunted a monosyllable and flicked his lighter into flame, applying it to his cigarette. He tapped the case by his side. "Do you want a cigarette?"

"No, thanks." She surveyed him

thoughtfully. "You're very quiet. Do you find all this rather boring, Andrew?"

"Wedding gifts? A little. It's your province rather than mine, isn't it?"

She crossed over to him and perched on the arm of his chair. "You'll have to live with them too, you know, my dear," she reminded him.

He raised an eyebrow. "I don't take very much notice of my surroundings, as a rule."

Sarah slipped an arm about his shoulders and brushed her lips across his cheek. "Not long to go now," she said lightly. "This is your last day as a bachelor, Andrew. Doesn't the thought fill you with apprehension?"

"Not at all," he replied smoothly.

Absently, she began to caress the dark hair which curled in small tendrils on the nape of his neck. "Do you think you'll like being married to me?" she asked. "I can be very difficult at times."

He smiled. "I know all there is to know about you, Sarah. I haven't any fears for the future. I've always known that you are the only woman I want for my wife—but I never thought you'd ever marry me." He raised a hand to clasp the restless fingers which twined themselves in his hair. His eyes searched her face anxiously and he was very still. "Sarah, you do know what you're doing?" he asked urgently. He caught the fleeting glance of impatience and he went on hastily: "I know you think that there's been too much talk, Sarah— but I want you to understand how important it is to me. Try to imagine my feelings if you decide within a few weeks or months that you made a mistake, that you can't be happy with me. I shall do everything in my power to make you happy—but happiness comes from within, my dearest. It still isn't too late to call the wedding off, Sarah—and believe me, I mean it when I say that I'd rather you changed your mind than married me only to regret it."

She was silent, studying the earnest expression of his handsome features, feeling the impact of his words. He made it sound so easy—and she was terribly tempted to admit that she did not want to marry him. The words actually trembled on her lips—and she was totally unaware that he read the truth in her eyes. He prepared himself for the pain of her next words.

Sarah desperately tried to muster the reasons why she did not want to marry him. Such a short while ago, it had seemed vitally important that she should be his wife and know herself safe in the harbour of his love and their long friendship. She still needed that safety and security. At least she would know peace of mind and the quiet contentment that the harmony of their understanding of each other had always ensured. Her fears of recent days seemed ludicrous now as she looked into his dark eyes, studied the familiar lines of his features, heard the echo of his pleasant, familiar voice still ringing in her brain with his offer of freedom. The strong clasp of his fingers was reassuring as was his warm, masculine nearness. She suddenly knew a surge of affection for him and she leaned forward to press her face against his hard, firm cheek. Her lips close to his ear, she murmured: "Put your arms about me, Andrew—hold me close. Hold me and never let me go!"

Her urgent words stirred him beyond expression. His arms drew her close into his embrace and she lay against him, silent, drawing new determination and strength from his nearness, resolutely blotting out her doubts and her memories of David with thoughts of Andrew's arms, Andrew's love.

"Say that you love me," she urged at last and her voice held a desperate appeal.

His arms tightened about her. "You know I love you," he said huskily. "I love you with all my heart—and I'll always love you, Sarah."

"No matter what happens?"

He raised a hand to smooth a silky tendril of hair from her face. "No matter what happens," he repeated as though it were a marriage vow.

"I don't want to change my mind," she whispered. "I wish it were already tomorrow—I wish we were married now!"

With pain tearing through him, Andrew recognised the desperation in her voice and knew that she sought to marry him only in the hope of forgetting her love for another man. He could not mistake the harsh urgency of her tone, the almost-painful grip of her arm about his neck, the rigid arching of her slim body. She was still in love with David Montrose, might always love him—yet she wanted to marry him almost as an escape. She wanted to put herself beyond the temptation of her love, her hopes and dreams. She did not know what she was doing—she was almost beside herself with disappointment and heartache and it seemed that she did not care what became of her life or her future if she could not have the man she loved. Yet Andrew knew he would not try to prevent her now. He had given her enough opportunities to retract—and she still clung to the desire to marry him. He would never be able to claim her love as his own—but he would be able to claim her as his wife and he decided that he was entitled to whatever happiness he could find in their marriage despite the knowledge which he must always carry with him.

Gently he sought her lips, as though to torment himself with her lack of response —but she kissed him eagerly, clinging to him with simulated ardour and begging him again to speak of his love for her. What strange satisfaction did she gain from that embrace, he wondered? What power did she know as she listened to his words of love? Did she merely seek reassurance that she was a woman who could inspire love in one man if not in the man she wanted? Did she really hope to find peace of mind in a marriage she had urged solely to prove to herself and to the man she loved that one man at least desired and needed her as his wife? He wondered what their life together would prove to be while she loved David Montrose and he was aware of that love and knew the futility of his own emotions.

Passionately, he resolved there and then that if it were possible he would force out the memory of David Montrose from her mind and heart and awaken a new love within her being—the love that was his right as her husband and his hope of many years.

Sarah sensed the new strength which permeated his entire being—and she raised herself and looked long into his face, seeking the answer to the determination she sensed in him. She was suddenly afraid for she felt that she looked into the face of a stranger. She missed the familiar warmth of his eyes, the easy curving of his lips into an affectionate expression, the tenderness of bone formation. His jaw-line had taken on a new strength, there was a grimness about his mouth and his eyes held a cold, steely resolution which puzzled her. Only a moment—and then the impression vanished but that moment was long enough for her to realise with a sinking heart that Andrew could never be deceived, that he would always know that she had married him while no vestige of love for him lived in her heart, that he was fully aware that only one man occupied all her thoughts and possessed all her emotions—and that man was not himself.

She said his name tentatively, almost fearfully, longing to erase the hint of reproach in his eyes and the faint light of contempt in his expression. She knew that he had every right to reproach and despise her—but she did not want to look at herself through his eyes. To marry him on the morrow would be to commit a grave offence against his integrity and his right to a wife who loved him—she would gain a husband but she would lose the friendship she had long cherished. Yet she would marry him, nevertheless—because their separate realisations of the truth remained unspoken and could never be discussed by them. Outwardly, they would behave as though the last few minutes had never been. He would not betray by word or expression that he knew her motives for marrying him: she would not reveal in any way her knowledge that he had seen through to the innermost depths of her being and certainly she would take care never to confirm or deny his unspoken accusations.

Her utterance of his name broke the tension and he smiled, glancing at his watch. "It's almost time for lunch," he said casually. He kissed her lightly and then helped her to her feet. She stood looking down at him for a long moment—then she returned his smile and knew that the first act of a play which would last a lifetime had just known the rising of the curtain.

7

SARAH came slowly down the staircase of her new home. The surroundings were familiar to her yet she looked about her with an air of bewilderment which owed itself to her inner turmoil. She felt lost and confused—and the sense of having made a terrible mistake was very strong in her that morning. She had taken pains with her appearance and before she left the large, beautifully furnished bedroom she looked at herself for a long moment as though she fully expected to meet the reflection of a stranger. But the same classical contours of features, the same clear, grey eyes and the same mop of auburn curls met her gaze. The difference was within her.

She hesitated with her hand on the panel of the breakfast-room door, wondering if Andrew waited for her on the other side and wondering how she would be able to face him with composure. A tiny shudder ran through her slim body as she vividly recalled the events of the previous night. Her wedding night . . .

She thought of Andrew's strong arms and his tender yet eager mouth seeking her lips, the murmured endearments and the barely-restrained passion of his firm, muscular body—the passion which she had so forcibly and involuntarily rejected as full realisation of her mistake dawned on her. She had been physically, mentally and spiritually incapable of responding to his ardour, of submitting to his embraces, for David's face was etched too clearly behind her closed eyes and the remembrance of his arms and his kisses had brought a tumult of tears. Andrew had been considerate and patient and understanding yet the look in his eyes had seared her heart. He had released her and gone from her room without another word—and now she reproached herself that she had not tried to prevent him, had not called him back. Instead she had buried her face in the pillow already wet with her tears and torn her emotions to shreds with futile yearning for David.

So much for her resolution to make a success of her life with Andrew! So much for her determination to forget David, in the arms of her husband! Her resolution and determination had weakened and melted away at the first questing touch of Andrew's lips—and now she knew that she would never cease to love David, never be able to forget him, never know happiness with Andrew or anyone else. She should not have married Andrew. She had no right to cause him humiliation and pain and she knew it was impossible for her to be the wife he wanted and merited. There was no room in her heart for anyone else but David and she could never give Andrew anything more than she had given him all these years—an easy friendship and a casual affection. It was not enough. How could it be enough when he loved her so much, when he had been so loyal and patient for such a long time, when he was prepared to accept her as his wife knowing how little she could give in return. He had still expected and hoped for more than she had found it possible to give—she had denied him the right to find ease and an ephemeral happiness in her arms and she had made it unmistakably clear to him that he would never take David's place in her life.

She did not hear her husband's approach and the sound of his voice startled her. She swung round and met the cool, determinedly-pleasant eyes. "Oh, there you are," she said obviously and inanely.

"Were you waiting for me?" he asked politely. He stretched his hand out to push open the door. "I didn't expect you to be down for breakfast, Sarah."

"It's such a lovely morning," she said, preceding him into the room. "It would have been a waste of the day to lie in bed any longer." She sat down in the chair which he pulled out for her and forced a tremulous smile of thanks to her lips. He pressed the bell-push which summoned his manservant and then seated himself opposite her at the table, picking up the newspapers and letters which were neatly stacked beside his place.

Throughout the meal, they exchanged polite conversation but the atmosphere was strained and Sarah merely toyed with the food which was set before her. At last she pushed away her plate and poured fresh coffee into her cup. She took a cigarette from her case and put it between her lips, lighting it with hands that trembled slightly. The meal was an ordeal which she could gladly have dispensed with. It seemed that Andrew meant to make no reference to the previous night and she felt incapable of making the apology which seemed so necessary. He was intent on his letters and took little notice of her. She felt so tensed that she longed to scream or throw something—anything to bring his attention back to her. Yet at the same time she was thankful for that lack of attention. She could not have borne recrimination or reproach or even discussion of the subject.

He looked up from his letters. "What would you like to do today, my dear?" he asked quietly.

"I thought our plans were made," she returned, a little sharply. "Lunch with the Denholms and tennis this afternoon—and dinner at home tonight."

He frowned slightly. "With your family," he amended. "You must remember that this is your home now, Sarah."

"I'm sorry—of course, Andrew," she said mechanically.

"You seem very subdued this morning," he remarked. "No one would believe that you were a radiant bride only yesterday. Didn't you sleep very well? Aren't you feeling well?"

Her chin tilted slightly. "I'm all right, thanks."

He smiled at her. "I suppose you're thinking about last night? Don't worry about it, my dear—it's not all that important."

She flushed slightly. "I'm afraid I behaved rather badly," she said quietly.

He touched her hand briefly with his own. "You'd had a long day. I expect you were tired and a little over emotional."

She stared at him in astonishment. Was that the line he meant to take? That she had merely been a distraught and somewhat nervous bride? When she knew beyond a shadow of doubt that he had been fully aware of the reason behind her instinctive rejection of him! Had he managed to find excuses for her behaviour which would salve his own wounded pride and allow them to take up the shattered

118

pieces of their marriage as though that terrible scene had never taken place? But Andrew was too direct, too forthright for pretence of that nature! He knew the truth and it was completely out of character for him to refuse to face it. Surely he must realise that their marriage didn't stand a chance of being successful! She would never be capable of responding to the passionate ardency of his nature!

As though the matter was closed and need not be reopened, he rose from his seat, gathering up his letters. "Excuse me, Sarah, won't you. I just want to scribble a few replies to these—but I won't be very long. I expect you'll find something to amuse you while I'm in the library— unless you want to glance through the papers and keep me company at the same time?"

"I'll come with you," she agreed, stubbing out her cigarette and rising eagerly to her feet. They could not leave matters at such an unsatisfactory stage. She must make it clear to him that unless her feelings underwent a violent change, she could never live with him as his wife in the fullest sense. She must know from his own lips whether he was prepared to continue with this farce of a marriage on those terms—or whether he would consider an annulment.

She found it extremely difficult to broach the subject to him. He wrote rapidly, occasionally referring to the papers on the desk beside him, glancing up to smile at her once or twice when he sensed her gaze upon him, seemingly engrossed in his occupation. Sarah skimmed idly and disinterestedly through the newspapers which contained references to their wedding on the previous day and brought fresh stabs of compunction. Her heart thudded unevenly and her brain evolved and rejected sentences which would bring about the necessary discussion of their circumstances. She was cold with apprehension and at the same time hot with embarrassment and humiliation. She plunged at last, forgetting her carefully-prepared speech. "Andrew—about last night . . ."

He looked up. "Well?"

His noncommittal reply was unhelpful but she went on, striving for coolness: "I'm sorry it was such a fiasco—but I must warn you that it's likely to happen again—and to go on happening."

His eyes narrowed. Carefully, he replaced the screw cap of his fountain pen and tidied the papers and letters before him. "I fail to understand why you should expect to burst into tears every time I come to your room at night, Sarah. Perhaps you'll enlighten me."

"Don't be so pompous!" she snapped, edgy and irritable. "This isn't easy for me to explain, Andrew."

With forefinger and thumb, he pulled thoughtfully at his underlip as he searched her expression. Then he said slowly: "There isn't any need for you to explain anything, my dear. Quite simply, you've no wish to be my wife in anything but the legal sense. Don't you think you made it clear enough last night? Don't you think I have some pride? You needn't worry, Sarah. It will be a long time before I attempt to make love to you again—if ever! The very thought of your unwillingness would cool any desire I had for you. I'm not a monster, after all—as you should know."

She clenched her hands until the finger-nails cut into the palms but she did not notice the pain. "Then you don't mind. . . ?" she asked hesitantly.

He rose abruptly and turned away so that she could not read his expression. He strode to the window and looked across the well-kept gardens. It was incredible that she could know so little about him, could lack so much perception and understanding. She had not married a stranger! She could not seriously imagine that he was indifferent to the warmth or otherwise of their marital relationship. She knew that he loved her. She must have sensed the storm of passion which her intoxicating beauty and nearness had roused in him on their wedding night. She was neither child nor fool! Yet she could ask him if he minded living with her as a celibate for an indefinite length of time! He thrust his hands deep into his pockets, battling against the anger and irrepressible contempt which swept through him. His hand encountered his much-loved old pipe which had often been his comfort—and he brought it out and thrust it between his strong white teeth, clenching hard on the stem as he fought for composure.

How did Sarah imagine he had spent the night? Sleeping peacefully and calmly without a care in the world? Bitterly he recalled the long, wakeful night while he tossed and turned in his lonely bed, his arms aching to hold the woman he loved and had the right to call his wife, his body racked with desire which tormented, his heart pained and grieving for the futility of his emotions and his thoughts whirling in a kaleidoscope of anger, sorrow, love, confusion and logic, pain and bitterness. How readily he had seized on excuses— and how reluctantly he had been compelled to admit the truth: that if his name and personality had been that of David Montrose, the night would have known a different and happier ending. He had ranted against the selfishness which had allowed her to give full rein to her disappointment and refuse to acknowledge his right to the small measure of happiness which she could bring him. In the next moment, he had asked himself if he could have found any joy in her embrace knowing that there was no love in her being for him. Did he want a dutiful wife —or an honest wife who found it impossible to pretend passion which did not exist?

The night sky was streaked with the first signs of daybreak before he eventually decided to exercise his patience and to make every effort to win her love before attempting to make her his wife in anything but name. It had been a difficult victory—and now it proved to be an empty one for he had recognised immediately that Sarah intended to issue an ultimatum: either she was his wife in name only and they continued with their marriage on those terms; or they could amicably arrange an annulment and endeavour to forget the mistake which both had made.

Sarah realised how foolish her words had been—and she studied his broad back with a tender compassion for his feelings in her eyes. Naturally he must mind. He was being considerate, as usual: had she ever known Andrew to be lacking in consideration or understanding? He knew how difficult it was for her to adjust herself to a new way of life. He knew how much she wished it were possible to forget David and to give her love to Andrew who deserved and had every right to happiness. No doubt he hoped that time would heal the still-bleeding wounds of her heart— and because he loved her, he must hope that one day she would learn to respond to that love. While that hope existed, he would not want an annulment of their marriage and it seemed that he was prepared, if not exactly content, to try to make something of their life together on the terms she suggested.

She went over to him and slipped her hand in his arm, feeling him tense beneath her touch. "Andrew, we have so many other things," she said gently. "Surely we can be happy together without . . ."

He looked down at her. "Of course we could—if you happened to love me very much. There are happy marriages in which a normal physical relationship is imposs- ible, of course—but the love has to be very great on both sides. We're both adult enough to realise that the majority of marriages would be complete failures if the physical factor was removed."

She spread out her fingers on his arm and studied the highly-polished, beautifully-kept nails. "Then you don't think that we have any chance of being happy, Andrew?"

He shrugged. "It's impossible to know that, my dear. Happiness is a very intangible quality, isn't it? Our separate conceptions of happiness are probably totally dissimilar. No doubt you are convinced that if you had married David Montrose you would have been perfectly happy— but you might have married him and known nothing but misery and regret."

Sarah flushed at the introduction of David's name. In a low voice, she said: "I thought you knew about David."

"I'm neither blind nor lacking in intelligence," he returned curtly. "I suspected it—and last night you confirmed my suspicions."

"What are you going to do?"

He looked down at her and amusement flickered briefly in his eyes. "What is there to do, Sarah? You're my wife now and I've no intention of releasing you from the marriage contract until we've given our marriage a reasonable chance. As I just pointed out to you, you might have married him and never known happiness. Only time will prove whether we can be happy together—with or without a normal married life."

"A reasonable chance," she repeated quietly. "What do you mean by that?"

He pursed his lips thoughtfully, considering her question. "I think a year or so will be long enough, don't you? If you find life intolerable with me and have the honesty to say so when we have been married a year, then we will take steps to have our marriage annulled. What you do after that is your affair, Sarah—but I doubt if you'll find Montrose waiting for you." He turned towards her, gripped her shoulders with his strong hands. "But I want your guarantee that you'll really try to find happiness with me. Don't take the attitude that you can stick it for a year as long as you have your freedom eventually."

She met his gaze levelly. "Very well, Andrew. In return I want your promise that you'll never mention David to me again. I want to forget him—but I'll never do so if you continue to sneer at him or remind me of my affair with him."

"I'd like to forget him too," Andrew returned and emotion gave a harshness to his voice. "I've no wish to remember that my wife is in love with another man—and that whenever I touch her she's thinking of him." She moved convulsively beneath his hands. "Oh, I don't blame you, Sarah," he went on in a gentler voice. "I knew what I was taking on when I married you . . ."

"And you regret it already?" she interrupted with a tiny catch in her voice.

He was silent, studying her lovely face, seized with the sudden impulse to draw her close, to kiss the soft, warm lips, to melt the ice in her heart and body that resisted his tender love. But the impulse died with the realisation that she would not welcome his embrace, that it would only serve to remind her of the man who was not her husband, that he would only lay himself open to fresh hurt. He must guard his vulnerable emotions—and his self-control was his only defence.

He released her shoulders abruptly. "No, I don't regret it," he told her. "I've wanted you for my wife for more years than I care to remember—I wanted you enough to take you on any terms and I haven't any real regrets. I love you, Sarah

—and like any man who loves, I have my hopes. I don't hope for your love any more. I realise that you can't give me that. But I do hope for a successful marriage and, oddly enough, I believe that in your heart you want our marriage to be a success. It will need patience and trust and affection on both sides. More than anything, it needs co-operation and I think you're willing to co-operate, Sarah."

She was moved by his quiet words and by the sincerity which lay behind them. "I'm more than willing, Andrew," she replied gently. She caught his hands eagerly and pressed them with her own. "Just leave things as they are for the time being," she added fervently. "I know it's very unsatisfactory—and scarcely fair to you—but it will be all right in time, I'm sure."

He returned the pressure of her hands and then released himself from her grasp. "A year," he reminded her. "I'll give you a year. I won't ask anything from you that you're not prepared to give, in that time. But at the end of a year—either we part amicably or you become my wife in the fullest sense of the word. I think you'll agree that I'm being as reasonable as I can be, in the circumstances."

She nodded swiftly. "More than reasonable, Andrew."

"Then there isn't any need to discuss the matter any longer," he said, returning to his desk and beginning to sort through the letters. "I must finish these. We'll soon have to leave for the Denholms so I suggest that you get ready." He sat down and picked up his fountain pen.

Sarah hesitated briefly, walked towards the door, then turned and came back. She stooped and kissed his cheek. There was a hint of penitence in the gesture—and a strange tenderness in her touch as she brushed the dark hair from his brow. He stiffened and stared unseeingly at the sheet of paper on which he had scrawled a few lines in his handwriting. He did not look up or acknowledge the affectionate caress in any other way—and Sarah sighed softly before she finally went from the room.

Alone, Andrew laid down his pen and closed his eyes, closing his mind at the same time to the memory of the strange, unnatural discussion which had taken place between them.

Sarah went back to her room and closed the door firmly behind her. She rested her back against the panels and relaxed, feeling the tension drain from her slowly as she considered Andrew's offer of a year's respite. A year: twelve months; surely it was long enough to recover from David and to know if there was any future in her marriage to Andrew. She did not pause to consider what lay beyond the end of that year. It was sufficient that she had twelve months in which to straighten out her emotions and to adjust herself to the knowledge that David could never have any place in her life in the future . . .

8

SARAH stretched out her hand to the telephone—and then withdrew it, bowing her head against the storm of temptation. How easy it would be to dial the familiar number! A matter of moments and she could hear again the much-loved voice which had the power to melt her resistance and stir her heart. What harm would it do? Who need ever know that she had been in touch with him? She was alone in London, having travelled up to spend a few days in a round of shopping, social calls and theatre visits. Andrew was unlikely to question how she had spent her time so there would be no need to lie to him. Besides, she only wanted to speak to David, to find out how he was, to learn if he remembered her as vividly as she remembered him. She would hurt no-one by getting in touch with him—and David had suggested himself that she should do so if she ever came to London. She knew that he still met Frances occasionally—but was it likely that he would mention her telephone call to Frances? Her cousin did not have a suspicious nature so even if she knew of the telephone call she would not think it odd that Sarah should contact an old friend. And David was an old friend, after all. They had been very close friends. Surely no one could object if she were to speak to him for a few minutes over an impersonal telephone wire!

The telephone shrilled—and her heart leaped. David? Then common-sense returned. Of course not. He did not know that she was in London and certainly he would not know that she was staying at the Gower Hotel. She picked up the receiver.

After a few moments while she waited to be connected with her caller, she heard Andrew's voice, clear and cool.

"Sarah? I thought I'd ring to find out if you arrived safely. How are you, my dear?"

She laughed softly. "I'm fine. It's only three hours since I left Avering—what could have happened to me?"

She could visualise his slow smile as he replied: "Quite a number of things in a big city. What was the journey like?"

"Not too bad. The train was a few minutes late."

"I'm telephoning from Kendrick House. Frances is travelling up to London this evening to spend a few days—she wanted to know where you were staying. I expect she'll be in touch with you."

Sarah's voice was suddenly sharp. "I didn't know that Frances had plans for a trip to Town. It wasn't your idea, Andrew?"

"My idea? I don't know what you mean."

He could not have faked the note of puzzlement in his voice and Sarah felt relief steal through her being. She must have been feeling guilty about the temptation to call David—else she would not have leaped so quickly to the suspicion that Andrew wanted her cousin to keep an eye on her while she was in London.

She managed to laugh lightly. "I thought you imagined I'd be lonely—and asked Frances to keep me company," she lied swiftly.

"Oh, I see. No, it's her own idea. I believe she intends to stay with friends." He went on: "You won't be lonely, surely?

I thought you had a great many plans for your time."

"I have!" she assured him gaily. "Don't be annoyed if I decide to stay longer than I planned, will you?"

"You know very well that I never interfere with your plans, Sarah," he returned quietly. "You come and go as you please. But don't stay away too long. I shall miss you."

Her voice softened. "Of course you won't. You're always too busy to notice if I'm around or not," she teased him gently. "Anyway, you should have come with me," she went on and there was a genuine note of reproach in her tone. "I wish you had, Andrew." She was sincere in that moment for she knew that nothing would prevent her from getting in touch with David and nothing would prevent her from agreeing if he suggested a meeting. She knew, also, that she was being foolish —yet something stronger than sense or loyalty urged her on. But if Andrew had accompanied her to London she would not have been able to telephone or meet David —and in that moment she sincerely wished that Andrew was present to nip temptation in the bud.

"You know that London doesn't appeal to me, my dear," Andrew replied. "But I would have come with you if you'd asked for my company. I thought you wanted a break. I thought you were looking forward to a few days away from me and Avering." He spoke lightly but with an undercurrent of meaning which Sarah could not fail to detect.

"I shall enjoy my stay in London—but I shall look forward to being home again," she told him deciding to ignore the implication of his words.

They talked for a few more minutes and then Andrew rang off. Slowly, Sarah replaced the receiver and looked at it thoughtfully. It was odd that Andrew should have telephoned her just when she had been on the point of ringing David's number. It was almost as though he had sensed the rising temptation and the indecision which tore through her and endeavoured to remind her of the loyalty she owed to him. Poor Andrew. Heaven knew he had little else but her loyalty and even that was teetering in the balance at the moment. She pulled her thoughts up sharply. She had no intention of being disloyal. All she wanted was the chance to speak to David for a few minutes—and perhaps the opportunity of meeting him for coffee or lunch. Nothing else. She was innocent of any other intentions so how could she be accused of disloyalty even in motive? Surely Andrew would not object to her wish to contact an old friend? Then she chided herself for self-deception. If Andrew discovered that she had been in touch with David again, he would be hurt and disappointed. She had promised to do all she could to forget David, to make a success of her life with Andrew—yet at her first opportunity she immediately thought of ways and means to renew her association with David.

She *had* tried to forget him. She had tried to replace his memory with thoughts of Andrew and his unfailing love and kindness and patience. Andrew was a good husband. She had been more content with him than she had thought possible. He had never made any demands on her and it had been easy to give him affectionate companionship. It had been a comfort to know that their friendship was unaffected by the circumstances of their difficult marriage. She still enjoyed his company and they had a pleasant, undemanding life together. She knew that he loved her but he did not make his love an irksome tie. He seldom spoke of his feelings and rarely gave any demonstration of the passion which burned consistently beneath his quiet, controlled demeanour. If they kissed, it was Sarah who brought about the embrace. She occasionally knew the impulse to put her arms about him and hold him close—but it was the impulse of affection and not of love. She knew that he sensed this and although he returned the warmth of her embrace and sought her lips when she offered them to him, he invariably released her within a few moments and made no attempt to carry matters further. She respected his self-control although she was feminine enough to be piqued sometimes and to wonder if he remained as unmoved as it seemed. There were times when she would have welcomed a closer relationship for she was a woman with a woman's needs and desires—but she was honest enough to admit to herself that if he had given any sign that he was growing impatient with their abnormal way of life, she would freeze once more. It was too soon. She was still too much in love with David to find any joy or pleasure in another man's arms. But she *had* tried to forget David. It was not her fault that the love she bore him was so powerful, so all-demanding. It had grown in strength during the months since she had lost him rather than abated. He was dearer to her now than ever before. The image of his handsome face and tall physique was clearer with every passing day. She found it easier to conjure up the memories of moments they had shared— which was ironic when she was so determined to push him out of her heart and mind.

Once again she stretched out her hand to the telephone and this time she did not reconsider. She gave the number decisively and waited for the connection. She listened to the ringing tone impatiently—and then it stopped. Her heart caught on a beat as David gave his number. Her mouth was dry and her mind went blank for a moment. Then he repeated the number and she said: "David? This is Sarah."

"Sarah!" The startled exclamation was followed by a swift, tender: "Sarah, how wonderful to hear from you. Where are you?"

"In London," she replied, smiling at the eagerness of his voice. "How are you, David?" She was hungry for news of him. The sound of his voice filled her with love and the sharp desire for his presence.

"I'm fine. How are *you?* And what are you doing in London?"

"Looking up some old friends," she replied lightly.

"I'm flattered that you remember me," he returned smoothly.

Her voice took on a new, reminiscent note. "How could I forget you, David?"

"Well, how's married life?" he asked teasingly.

Her cheeks burned. "Need we discuss that?"

"I quite agree with you," he said and he laughed softly. "Where are you staying?"

"At the Gower Hotel."

"Excellent. Near enough for me to be with you in less than ten minutes. You're going to have lunch with me, of course. I'll meet you in the Cocktail Lounge, Sarah."

The line went dead and she slowly replaced the receiver on its cradle. He hadn't changed at all. He was as forceful, as confident, as he had always been. Taking command of the situation, immediately assuming that she would want to see him and making arrangements for a meeting without consideration of any plans she might have already made. With a singing heart, she almost ran to the dressing-table and carefully powdered a nose that was far from shiny. She ran a comb through her curls, rearranged an ear-ring, tugged at her skirt, changed her shoes and handbag—and then restlessly paced the room, smoking a cigarette she did not want, until she could go down to the Cocktail Lounge to meet David in good time.

He was there already, as she had known he would be. He was seated on one of the tall stools at the bar, chatting to the attractive barmaid yet watching the reflection of all who entered in the mirrors which lined the wall of the bar. He spun round as she walked through the swing doors and smiled—that warm, easy smile which went straight to her heart and brought an instinctive, responsive curve to her lips.

He moved to greet her and their hands touched in the old, intimate manner. Then he suggested that she should sit at a table in a discreet corner while he procured drinks for them both. Sarah went to sit down and as she waited, she studied him intently, aware that the magic of his personality was again casting its potent spell. Her eyes were warm with tenderness and her love for him blazoned its declaration as she watched and waited on his every movement.

He joined her, placing the drinks on the table. He sat beside her and half-turned to smile. "As beautiful as ever," he said lightly. "I can't believe you're really here. I thought you'd walked out of my life for ever." He laid his hand over hers. "I've missed you, Sarah."

"And I've missed you," she said, endeavouring to speak as lightly but aware that the warmth in her eyes betrayed the intensity of her feelings.

His hand tightened on hers with a convulsive movement. "For God's sake,

142

Sarah—if you look like that, I shall be tempted to kiss you here and now."

"David!" She tried to convey shocked amusement. "I'm a respectable married woman," she reminded him.

"What's a kiss between friends!" he returned.

She laughed shakily. "You haven't changed, my dear."

His eyes narrowed slightly. "You have —but I suppose three months of marriage changes most women." His voice altered as he went on: "I expected to hear from you before, Sarah. Is this your first trip to Town since you were married?"

Sarah nodded. "Yes." She looked at him sharply. "You knew I would get in touch with you?"

He smiled impudently. "Of course. I know you, Sarah—remember? You were always capable of justifying your actions and if your conscience pricked just a little when you telephoned me, I'm sure you stifled it with the argument that it wasn't necessary to neglect old friends just because you're a respectable married woman." His words were teasing and true enough to bring the faintest colour to her cheeks. He brought out his cigarettes and offered them to her. She was glad to bow her head over the flame of his lighter—the momentary respite cooled her features and restored the composure he had shaken. "As we are old friends," he went on, studying the glowing end of his cigarette, "perhaps you'd tell me why you married Whitaker in such a rush? You see, I find it difficult to believe that you suddenly realised that you loved him—you loved me and no one changes in such a brief period of time."

"Perhaps I didn't really love you," she retorted, playing for time.

He shook his head, that slow smile curving his lips.

"You loved me," he repeated and his tone brooked no argument. "But your patience ran out."

"I waited so long," she said swiftly, breathlessly.

His smile implied his understanding and a warm reassurance. "Yes, I know. I treated you very badly, my lovely Sarah. I'll admit that willingly. But I've had plenty of opportunities to realise how stupid I was where you were concerned."

She turned to him eagerly. "What do you mean, David?" It was blessed relief to speak his name without fear or guilt. She thought of the many times she had uttered it aloud in the long hours of the night, wondering if some telepathic force could convey the depths of her love to him across the miles and bridging the gulf which separated them.

He shrugged. That tiny movement of his broad shoulders implied that he half-regretted his frankness and at the same time saw no reason why he should hide the truth any longer. Abruptly he said: "This is ridiculous—sitting here, making conversation and pouring drinks we don't really want down our throats, when all I want is you in my arms and a little privacy. I should have come up to your suite, Sarah."

She caught her breath. "David. . . ?"

He caught hold of her fingers and pressed them to his lips. There was an ardency in the gesture which caused her heart to leap with a joyful hope. "I love you, Sarah," he said, so quietly that she wondered for a shattering second if she had really heard the words. "I've always loved you."

"No!" The exclamation was forced from her. The blood was suddenly chilled in her veins and her heart seemed to miss a beat. Life could not be this cruel!

"But you knew that, Sarah," he said quietly.

"I didn't know . . ." she protested.

"Surely it was obvious that you were the only woman for me—all I'd ever want? I just didn't want to be tied down too soon. I like to move at my own pace and you wanted to rush me into marriage. I would have married you eventually and I thought you loved me enough to wait."

"You made it very obvious that you didn't want to marry me!" she snapped with a flash of anger.

He ran a hand through his crisp blond hair. "I expect it did seem like that to you."

"I asked you point-blank if you meant to marry me—and you shook your head and said no," she reminded him painfully.

"You were too intense about it. You made it seem a matter of life and death—and I wasn't going to be forced into anything, darling. I like to do the hunting —and I was annoyed at the time by your insistence. I thought a few months' break from each other wouldn't hurt either of us. I believed in your love and I knew I wanted you—but on my terms."

She was silent, thinking of his words. At last she said slowly: "Rather a selfish point of view, David."

"Perhaps. I couldn't know that you'd marry Whitaker in a fit of pique. I doubt if I would have acted any differently had I known that, anyway. I'm not the type to be bludgeoned into anything—certainly not marriage."

"Pride and nothing else!" she snapped.

"Well, you're married now—for better or worse," he told her. He picked up his glass and drained the contents.

"And if I wasn't?" She searched his expression, her eyes suddenly eager with renewed hope. Her anger against him faded: she had never been able to withstand the charm of his personality and her love for him now was stronger than the pain of his arguments.

He touched her cheek with a gentle fore-finger. "That would be a different story,

Sarah." He indicated her glass. "Drink up, darling. Let's find a restaurant and have some lunch." His abrupt change of mood did not startle or surprise her for she had known his every mood at one time and she was familiar with his effervescent nature.

As they left the Cocktail Lounge of the hotel, she said impulsively: "David, we could lunch in my suite. I'll telephone to Room Service."

He hesitated briefly, then took her elbow and urged her towards the lifts. "Sensible girl—good food and privacy. What more do we want?"

As they entered her suite, Sarah knew a strange trepidation in the pit of her stomach. David closed the door with an odd little sound of finality and the next moment she was in his arms and his lips sought hers with passionate, demanding ardour. Briefly she resisted him and then she trembled in his embrace, answering the urgency of his kisses with all the intensity of her love. She had dreamed so often of a moment like this and his nearness caused her senses to swim. She forgot the intervening months, forgot that she was married to Andrew, forgot everything but her love for David and her joy in the newly-discovered knowledge that he loved her in return.

"Do you really love me?" she asked, against his lips, knowing but wanting further assurance.

"I love you," he murmured. "I love you, Sarah. There'll never be anyone but you."

Caught in his arms, ensnared in the spell he wove, listening to the beloved voice speaking the words she had longed to hear, her heart overflowed with love for him and time stood still. And then came the memory that she was married to Andrew and that their love could never bring them any happiness. David had spoken too late.

"Don't say that!" she cried brokenly. "Oh, David—don't say that! You mustn't love me—you mustn't! It's too late!" She began to sob and he drew her face against his shoulder, running his fingers through her hair, soothing her with endearments. "Why didn't you tell me before?" she demanded. "David, darling David—it's too late now!"

"I know," he murmured. "I'm the only

one to blame, Sarah. I know it's too late but there's no sin in loving you—and if there were, I couldn't change the way I feel about you. Kiss me, Sarah!" he pleaded with sudden urgency and she turned her face to him, seeking to hold him ever closer, her resistance melting in the passion of his embrace.

He lifted her easily in his arms and carried her to the long settee. He laid her down gently and stood looking at her for a few moments. Sarah's heart thudded painfully. If they loved each other, surely they had the right to take whatever happiness was offered to them. She moved so that he could sit beside her and held out her arms to him. To her dismay and astonishment, he shook his head and turned away.

"No more kissing, Sarah," he said gently. "Time to talk."

She wrinkled her forehead in a tiny frown. "What about, darling?"

"About us, of course." He smiled tenderly, as though she were a child. "You didn't want to discuss your marriage, but I must know if you're happy. Do you regret marrying Whitaker?"

Sarah hesitated. Was she happy? She was not actively unhappy. Did she regret her marriage? It was difficult to be certain. In all truth she could not say that she was unhappy with Andrew for she had found a strange contentment with him that left little room for real regret. She always carried in her heart the secret of her love for David and the wish that he could have been her husband—but at the moment her marriage was working out extremely well: partly because it was based on years of close friendship and warm regard, partly because Andrew's patience and consideration made it easy for her to stifle the feeling that she was being unfair to him.

A shadow touched David's eyes briefly. "Your silence is my answer," he said quietly. "That's all I wanted to know."

9

WHEN David left her, after they had lunched together in an atmosphere of strained efforts to pick up old threads without dwelling upon the closeness of their past relationship, Sarah was able to review the tumultuous couple of hours in his company. While he was with her, thoughts and emotions had whirled incoherently and now she felt tired and drained, needing a breathing space to marshal her thoughts into some semblance of order and quietude. She had promised to dine with him that evening at a night-club which had once been a favourite haunt—and she looked forward to being with him again yet at the same time she half-regretted that she had contacted him so impulsively.

She knew that he loved her but the knowledge did not bring the joy and pleasure that she felt it should. In her heart, there was the faintest of doubts that his love could prove as lasting and as worthwhile as the love which Andrew gave so unstintingly. Her spirits were low as she recalled her heartbroken cry that he had spoken too late. She must always be racked with visions of what might have been if only he had not been so proud, stubborn and so reticent with regard to his feelings. Or if only she had not rushed into marriage with Andrew. But it was futile to cite "ifs". They were both to blame for he had been too cautious and she had been too impetuous. She thought of his outspoken reminder that he was a man who preferred to do the hunting—and her cheeks flushed as she realised that throughout their association she had always been the one to force the pace, to admit impulsively that she loved him, to bring up the subject of their future and a possible marriage. But if David had loved her, then there would have been no need for such measures on her part—and she wondered if it were true that he had always loved her or whether he was simply the type of man who could convince himself that he was in love when the woman he wanted was not in a position to marry him and take away his freedom.

She paced the room restlessly, smoking a cigarette, thinking of David for the first time in a somewhat cynical light—and comparing him with Andrew. David was amusing, gay and lovable with a personable charm and manner—but he lacked the worthwhile qualities of Andrew's character and temperament. Or so it seemed to Sarah and she was a little taken aback to discover that the real David did not live up to the mental image which had kept her love alive for the last six months.

She still loved him: it seemed impossible that any man could ever take his place in her heart. She loved him so much yet she was no longer so blind to his imperfections. Because Andrew had proved himself to be an excellent husband in every way, it did not follow that he could oust the memory of David or win her heart. No one could love to order, she told herself rebelliously.

But following swiftly on the heels of that thought came another—she could stifle the impulsive urges of her love for David and try to make Andrew a happier man. On principle alone, that was her obvious course to take for there was little future in loving David. After all, she had married Andrew and she owed him some consideration and loyalty. Too, she had been strangely content with Andrew and in three short months they had built something between them which she could not fail to appreciate—an understanding, a warmth and affection, an intimacy of mind and spirit. She tried to imagine a future without Andrew—and then she tried to visualise David in the rôle of her husband and found it impossible to do so. Despite all her efforts, the image of Andrew still persisted as though it were deeply etched on her mind. No doubt the logical explanation was that David had always impressed upon her that he was not a marrying man—and Andrew was so obviously a man who needed a wife and family to complement him.

A sudden thought crossed her mind and she stubbed out her cigarette violently. How would David react if she told him of her agreement with Andrew and pointed out that if he really loved her she could obtain her freedom in order to marry him? It might be a year or more before they could be together but surely the waiting would be an excellent test of the strength of his love. His reactions would serve to tell her if his declaration of love was sincere: if he loved her, he would want to marry her and eagerly seize on the opportunity provided by Andrew's suggestion of a year's trial and eventual annulment of their marriage if she wished it; if he did not love her, she would know immediately by any hesitation or reluctance on his part. Her spirits soared as the idea took more concrete form. He must love her. She could not believe that his recent display of emotion owed itself to anything but love.

If he had not so determinedly steered clear of the subject when she had failed to reply to his questions regarding her marriage, she might have mentioned the agreement to him during lunch. But it had been too difficult to re-open the subject which obviously caused him pain and she had not wished to mar their reunion by discussing her impetuous marriage to Andrew. But they were meeting that evening and she would create the opportunity to sound him on the possibility of a shared future . . .

With her mind made up and her heart

lighter as she happily contemplated a hopeful reaction from David, she was able to make plans for her afternoon and carry them out in good humour.

She returned from a shopping spree and an informal tea-party with some girl-friends with just enough time to bath and change before David arrived at the hotel. He was punctual and she opened the door to his knock, flushed with anticipation, her eyes bright and looking particularly beautiful in a cocktail dress of ice blue grosgrain. The warm admiration which sprang to his eyes was reward for the pains she had taken with her appearance. He caught her by the shoulders and drew her towards him. Unresisting, she gave herself up to the sweet joy of his kiss.

"Still love me?" he murmured against her lips.

She drew away slightly, her eyes teasing as she met his ardent gaze. "You're leaping to conclusions, aren't you, David? Did I say that I was still in love with you?"

His arms tightened about her. "You never needed to put it into words, my lovely Sarah. Your lips and your eyes are expressive enough. Do you think I don't know how you feel about me? Did you think you could hide your love from me when it was written all over you as you saw me again this morning?"

She placed her cheek against his. "Yes, I love you, David," she said softly.

His lips brushed her throat and then he said intensely: "Enough to leave your husband and chance your happiness with me, Sarah?"

She could not understand the involuntary hesitation she felt—but the thought of Andrew came rushing to her mind and she knew how deeply hurt he would be by such an action on her part and how little he deserved to be hurt. Then in a rush of words, she cried: "You mean—now?"

"Of course. Don't go back to him. Stay here in London with me, darling," he urged.

She released herself from his embrace and walked across the room to a table on which stood some decanters. Thoughtfully, she poured drinks for them both and then came back to him. She handed him a glass. "You really mean it, David?"

He nodded. He lifted the glass to his lips, threw back his head and drained the contents. "I've thought of nothing else all afternoon," he told her frankly. "It seems to be the only way out. You wouldn't answer me when I asked if you were happy —at the time I believed that I'd made a mistake about the way you feel about me. I decided that in spite of everything you must be happy with Whitaker—in which case there wasn't any chance for me. But, thinking it over, I realised that it wasn't a fair question. How could I doubt that you still loved me? But obviously you wouldn't admit that you'd made a mistake in marrying Whitaker in case I suspected that you wanted me to do something about it. Well, I do want to do something about it —I want you to leave him and live with me. He'll divorce you, I suppose, and we'll see what happens then."

"Wait a minute, David," she told him. "Give me a cigarette, darling, will you?" He brought out his case and complied with her request. She took his glass and refilled it. He watched her, silent, studying her pensive expression. She perched on the arm of a comfortable chair and then said: "We have an agreement—Andrew and I —that I can have my freedom if I wish after we've been married for a year. If I left him now, he might refuse to give me a divorce. But if I keep to the agreement, then I should be free to marry you, David —and it isn't really very long to wait."

He frowned. "You have an agreement? Why? Was it your suggestion so that you'd have everything on your side if things worked out just as they have?"

"No." She did not meet his eyes. Intent on a scrutiny of the glowing end of her cigarette, she said: "It's difficult to explain, David. Our marriage isn't like any other. You see, Andrew has always known that I'm in love with you but he hopes I shall forget you. He's given me a year. If I'm still in love with you when the year is up—as I shall be, of course—I can have my freedom and he'll know that at least we tried to make a success of our marriage."

David raised an eyebrow. "Very magnanimous on his part. The man's either a fool or too much in love to see straight. I'm damned if I'd marry any woman on those terms."

"Andrew isn't a fool," she said quietly and realised as she spoke the words how true they were. For the first time it dawned upon her that if she had not contacted David she would probably never have met him again and when she had been married to Andrew for a year, their marriage would have been too valuable to them both to destroy—and Andrew would have achieved that result by his patience, his kindness and consideration, his generosity and the strength of his love. Even now, with the chance of happiness with David, there was still the possibility that she would prefer to remain married to Andrew who had proved his worth as a husband. Only time would provide the answer . . .

"Then he's in love with you," David said curtly and she pulled her thoughts back to the present. "Well, that's understandable, I suppose. Do you really think he'll release you without any protest after a year of living with you, Sarah?"

She nodded. "Oh yes, I know he will." Andrew was too honourable to break their agreement, she told herself. He loved her enough to sacrifice his own happiness for her sake. She thought of David's innate selfishness which she had always deplored but accepted because she loved him and

161

because he had so many charms which outweighed that one great fault. Was it possible that such a selfish man could truly love anyone more than himself or was capable of consistent giving as Andrew had proved to be? Hastily she dismissed the thoughts of disloyalty to the man she loved and went on eagerly: "It isn't very long, is it, darling? Not even a year! Surely we can wait—if we love each other enough."

He helped himself to a fresh cigarette and tapped it on his thumbnail, his eyes thoughtful. "I'm not sure that I care to wait, Sarah. I want you now—and if you love me enough, you'll leave Whitaker without any hesitation."

She rose swiftly and went to him, putting her arms about him. "David, I can't! I promised Andrew to live with him for a year! You wouldn't make me break my word, surely? I love you but I can't walk out on Andrew just like that. It wouldn't be fair to him. You don't know him—you don't know how good he's been to me, how much I owe him. Besides, our happiness wouldn't be worth very much if we took it at his expense."

His eyes narrowed and he released

himself from her embrace. "I don't see the logic of your arguments, Sarah. Whitaker will be the one to suffer, anyway, whether now or in a year's time."

That was so true and a wave of compassion for Andrew swept over her. But it was not as strong as the heady intoxicant of her love for David and she argued swiftly:. "I know that but at least he'll have had a year of happiness with me."

"A strange sort of happiness—sitting on a volcano waiting for the eruption. He must know that you're still in love with me, Sarah. Do you think he won't sense your impatience to be free? What manner of man is he that he'd hold on to you until the end of a year when it's a question of your happiness? If he loves you, he'll let you go now without a fight."

Sarah wondered briefly if that would be Andrew's reaction—in the same moment, she knew that because he loved her he would make every effort to hold on to her even though he might be well aware of the hopelessness of his efforts.

"If you really want to be fair to him, you'll tell him the truth now and ask for your freedom," David continued. "In any case, Sarah, you forget one detail—neither you nor Whitaker could file a petition for divorce until three years after the date of your marriage. That makes the waiting period rather longer than you anticipate . . ."

She interrupted him swiftly. "That isn't necessary in the case of an annulment," she retorted.

He caught her by the shoulders. "Annulment?"

Sarah nodded. "I'm only Andrew's wife in name—nothing else. That was part of the agreement."

He looked long and searchingly into her eyes until something in his gaze caused her to drop her lashes. She felt strangely uncomfortable. Surely she had not read a faint contempt in the depths of his blue eyes?

"Now I understand why you claimed your marriage isn't like any other," he said slowly. "The poor devil! A year with you on those terms—and nothing afterwards for all his patience. I'm surprised that you fell in with such a suggestion, Sarah. Don't you think that Whitaker is entitled to anything but the empty privilege of calling you his wife?"

"Why should you worry about Andrew?" she demanded impatiently. "It was his decision—and if you must know, I was thankful that he didn't make any demands on me. Do you think I could have lived with Andrew as his wife in every way when I love you so much?"

"You married him, didn't you?" he asked and his tone was cold. "What did you expect? If the idea of sleeping with him was so repugnant to you why on earth did you marry him in the first place?"

His blunt words brought a swift colour to her cheeks. "I suppose I didn't think about that aspect of marriage," she said quietly. "There wasn't much time . . ."

"Don't talk such utter rubbish!" he exclaimed irritably. "Of course there was time. What you really mean is that you backed out at the last minute. Good lord! If you had treated me like that, I should have made it very clear that as your husband I expected to share your bed—and the sooner you grew used to the idea the better."

"Must we discuss it?" she asked, lifting

her chin in a gesture of defiance. "Anyway, my marriage could be annulled without any difficulty—and surely that pleases you. It means that I can get my freedom and marry you . . ."

"You're as impetuous as ever, aren't you?" he asked with a slow smile. "Think back, Sarah. Have I asked you to marry me yet?"

She was stunned. She stared at him, trying to gauge his mood, to discover if he was serious or flippant, but his blue eyes were inscrutable as he met her gaze levelly. "But you asked me to leave Andrew?"

"That's right—but I didn't suggest marrying you. You carried it on from there, my lovely Sarah," he reminded her.

She forced a smile to stiff lips. "But you . . . but that's what you meant!"

"Are you so sure?"

"Then—what did you mean?" she demanded.

"It's very unwise to leap to conclusions, darling," he told her lightly. "But that was always one of your faults. I asked you to leave Whitaker and live with me—and now I'll add that if we're happy together,

I'll marry you when you get your freedom."

She breathed a sigh of relief. Then something about his last words struck her forcibly and she was suddenly sick with apprehension. "And if we're not happy together. . . ?"

"Then I wouldn't marry you, naturally," he pointed out. "I've too much sense."

"But that's a ridiculous suggestion!"

"Why? I think it's an extremely practical suggestion. Supposing we hate the sight of each other in three months? Supposing we do nothing but quarrel? Or supposing you decide that you prefer Whitaker to me? If we were married, it would entail all the ugliness of a divorce. Whereas if we merely lived together we could part on friendly terms and go our separate ways. However, we'd give it a trial—a year, for instance. If we were happy, we'd get married. It's as simple as that, Sarah."

"But it's such a risk," she objected, struggling to frame words for the instinctive repugnance to his ideas that she knew.

"So is marriage," he pointed out.

"Which is so difficult to escape from—in normal circumstances, of course. After all, Sarah, I'm only asking you to break your agreement with Whitaker and enter into a new one with me. There isn't much difference between them, in actual fact—except that Whitaker was honourable enough to marry you and that I wouldn't be content with a celibate relationship!"

"You can't be serious, David?" She looked up at him, searching in vain for the light of mischief she hoped to find in his eyes. She saw nothing but granite resolution and then she knew that he was in deadly earnest. She was shocked and incredulous. "But you are," she said slowly.

"That's right."

"I couldn't possibly agree . . ." she began.

"Then you don't love me enough—or at all," he told her. "Perhaps you're really in love with your husband?" It was a mocking question.

She closed her eyes against the swelling of pain. "David, don't be cruel! You know I love you—more than anything else in the world!"

"Then the mere formality of marriage houldn't worry you," he pointed out. 'It's a man-made institution, after all. It's a fifty-fifty chance, my lovely Sarah—and ou used to enjoy gambling."

"Fifty-fifty chance?" she repeated, vrinkling her brow in an effort to understand him.

"Of course. I might marry you—and again I might not. We might be happy—and we might not. Come, Sarah, I thought you were the unconventional type."

"I'm thinking of Andrew," she retorted honestly. "Not the conventions!" It was true. Her first thought had been for Andrew's contempt if she took such a step —and his disappointment in her morality and integrity. How could she ever hold up her head again if she agreed to David's suggestions?

He smiled and replied smoothly: "I suppose you realise that you're putting your husband before me yet you claim to love me more than anything else in the world!"

"Because I haven't any choice. I married Andrew and I promised to stay with him for a year. It's going to be unpleasant

169

enough breaking the news to my family and all my friends when I eventually leave him to marry you—can't you imagine how humiliating it would be for Andrew if I walked out on him after three months."

He shook his head. "You're thinking of yourself—not Andrew. You're afraid of what your family and friends would think and say about you, Sarah. Your concern isn't for your husband at all. I'm surprised at you, darling. But we won't argue any more. The subject's closed . . ."

"But we love each other!" she cried and she stretched out her hand to him blindly. "I'll never be happy without you—and how could you be happy without me, David? We love each other!"

"That seems to be our misfortune," he returned drily. He drew her close to him and once again she knew his lips upon her mouth. His arms were strong and urgent and she knew the tension of his body as his kiss became more insistent and passion rose swiftly within him. A strange dread sprang to life but it was completely disassociated from David. It was almost as though she knew a premonition of an unhappiness greater than she had ever known. Her body trembled and she knew a strange icy coldness in her veins and her heart thudded violently. "Relax, darling," David murmured gently, misconstruing her panic-stricken attempts to release herself from his embrace. "I'm not going to hurt you. My lovely Sarah . . ."

Abruptly they sprang apart as someone rapped lightly on the door of the room. They looked at each other—and Sarah wondered fleetingly if her own expression was as guilty as David's.

"Who the devil . . . ?" he began.

She spread her hands in a negative gesture. Then she crossed to the door and opened it, forgetting that her appearance was far from as immaculate as when David had arrived. With a sense of shock and dismay, she faced Andrew—and barely noticed the slim figure of her cousin in the background . . .

10

THE smile which touched Andrew's lips and gave a tenderness to his expression faded abruptly. "I brought Frances up to Town . . ." He broke off as he caught sight of her companion. A look of bewilderment crept into his eyes—and then they hardened to steel. Almost instinctively he knew the identity of the man who met his eyes with something akin to insolence in his own gaze. Coolly polite, so icy as to chill Sarah's entire being, he went on: "I'm sorry, Sarah—I thought you would be alone."

Before she could reply, Frances said quickly, a note of astonishment in her voice: "Why, David! This is a surprise." She threw Sarah a puzzled half-accusing glance and then turned to Andrew with a hint of compassion in her eyes.

Sarah stepped forward impulsively. "This is an old friend—David Montrose.

David, this is my husband, Andrew Whitaker."

A tiny nerve jumped in Andrew's cheek. His keen eye noticed the smudged lipstick, the disarranged curls and the guilt in his wife's eyes. He was filled with a cold and terrible anger, knowing a violent urge to strike her despite the appeal in her eyes that he should not cause a scene which could only prove humiliating to everyone. With an effort he controlled himself and nodded curtly to the other man.

David stretched out his hand. "How are you?" He smiled with easy affability. "I've been looking forward to meeting you, Whitaker. Sarah has told me so much about you." He was perfectly at his ease: a little amused by the situation and wondering what would happen next.

Andrew ignored the conventional gesture. "I had no idea that Sarah was still in touch with you," he said coldly.

David grinned. "She telephoned me this morning and I was delighted to hear from her. Since your marriage, she seems to have cut herself off from all her friends. I suggested we should have dinner together to talk over old times—you've no objection, I hope?" He went on smoothly, without giving Andrew time to reply: "We were just leaving, as a matter of fact."

"Then we arrived at an opportune moment," Andrew returned curtly. "Very good of you to take so much trouble, Montrose. I should have travelled with Sarah earlier but I was delayed—as it happens, I managed to get away this evening, after all."

Sarah moved to the decanters and clattered them in an attempt to break the tension. "Andrew, a drink? Frances? David, I know you'll have another . . ." She forced a smile to her lips but she was filled with trepidation. There was something about the steeliness of Andrew's eyes which filled her with dread. She could sense the jealousy in her cousin's attitude and she realised that Frances had grown to care for David during the last few months when she had met him on several occasions. She knew that David was ill at ease despite the affable smile which curved his lips and his apparent nonchalance. She busied herself with pouring the drinks although no one had accepted her offer.

David turned to Frances with a smile.

"How are you, Frances? I didn't expect you to be in London until tomorrow."

"I changed my plans," she returned mechanically. Her eyes were reproachful.

"Perhaps we could all dine together?" he suggested with an imp of mischief sparking in his blue eyes.

Frances said quickly: "I think Sarah and Andrew might prefer to be alone."

He nodded. "I expect you're right." He smiled at Sarah. "You'll forgive me for crying off, Sarah, won't you? We must have dinner together another time. Frances, will you take pity on me and have dinner with me?"

She demurred swiftly. "I'm afraid I already have an appointment, David. But I would appreciate it if you would run me to my friends' place?"

"Certainly," he agreed readily.

Sarah carried the drinks over to them. "Have a drink, first," she insisted, adopting a composure she did not feel. She handed them each a glass. Her hand brushed against her husband's and she looked up at him apprehensively. He refused to meet her gaze and she knew a stab of pain although she fully understood

175

his feelings and realised that she had only herself to blame for the anger which burned beneath his icy calm.

Frances sipped her drink, studying David and Sarah from beneath lowered lashes. She was angry with her cousin that she should have arranged a clandestine meeting with David at her first opportunity—but she saw no reason to mar her swiftly-developing friendship with David by being angry with him. She had no right to show jealousy, after all: no right to question his actions; who could blame him if Sarah had contacted him and forced him into the dinner invitation. No doubt he had acted purely from motives of friendship and old association. She knew that David was not really in love with Sarah: he had allowed himself to exaggerate the strength of his feelings because it pleased him to desire a woman who was unattainable. Frances was convinced that one day he would find all he sought in a woman in her own character and personality—until then she could be patient for since she had known his friendship and warm charm she had fallen in love with him and known that her old feeling for Andrew had been based merely on a lonely need to love and be loved. It seemed that she knew David's character very well and because she sensed that he shrank from eager possessiveness or too warm an interest, she kept their association on a deliberately cool standing and knew that he was intrigued by her reticence and reserve.

For a few moments, David kept the conversational ball rolling, receiving only curt and cold response from Andrew and half-hearted encouragement from Sarah. He finished his drink and turned to Frances. "Ready?" He caught Sarah's eyes and smiled at her reassuringly. "It was pleasant to meet you again, Sarah—I hope you won't make the mistake of burying yourself in the country again. I shall look forward to meeting you and your husband whenever you come to London—you know where to reach me."

Andrew flashed him a look of icy contempt and then turned his gaze back to the contemplation of his drink. He scarcely acknowledged the courteous farewell spoken by David but he followed the man's progress from the room with eyes that were steely with anger.

Sarah reached for a cigarette and lighted it with hands that shook a little. The sound of the door closing behind her cousin and David brought fresh apprehension and she prepared herself for the storm of accusation. She wished she did not feel so guilty. If only her meeting with David had been as innocent as he had implied, she would have no fears, able to refute accusation with a clear conscience. But she remembered David's kisses, the hard strength of his arms, the murmured endearments and her willingness to recall the past and recapture ecstasy that was gone for ever—and suddenly she despised herself.

Andrew was very still and ominously silent. He had moved away from her and stood at the window, looking down on the busy pavement below. He did not look at her or make any move towards her and the tension was almost unbearable. She was very conscious of the pain which he strove to conquer and knew that she had dealt him an unforgivable blow—both to his heart and to his pride. He had trusted her —and she had betrayed that trust without a qualm or a thought for the loyalty he had every right to expect from her. She drew nervously on her cigarette, waiting, waiting . . .

She was flooded with a wave of tenderness and regret which startled her by its intensity. Dear good Andrew—she had not meant to hurt him by her impulsive actions. As she studied his broad, uncompromising back, she realised how much her affection for him had deepened and strengthened in the three months of their marriage—and she also realised that her life had been enriched in many ways by his great love for her.

She had been not only foolish but criminally childish in her actions. It had been absolute folly to contact David. The past was the past and could never be recaptured. The present and the future revolved around Andrew and she should make him her first consideration—it was an additional burden on her conscience that she had the knowledge that Andrew was incapable of a similar action. His integrity was undeniable and admirable and his loyalty unshakable. She had proved herself to be untrustworthy—more than that, unworthy of his love and for the first time she considered what it would mean to her if he took away the support, the comfort and the strength of his love. A shaft of pain left her breathless as she realised how empty her life would be . . .

She had always known that while David remained a part of her past, she could find contentment with Andrew—yet she had deliberately sought to bring him back into her life merely through a selfish desire to satisfy the need which was brought about by her love for him. But did she really love him? It was more than possible that she had been in the grip of a mad, passionate infatuation, hypnotised by his charm, flattered by his interest—an infatuation which seemed now to be dead and empty. If it was love, would she have been so content with Andrew? Could she even have contemplated marrying him in the first place? Would she have shrunk so instinctively from David's suggestion that she leave Andrew and live with him? Surely she would have snatched at the chance of happiness, even on such an insecure and unsatisfactory basis, and considered the world well lost for love. Certainly she would not have been so dismayed to find him capable of such a suggestion—or so shocked to discover that he was able to dismiss Andrew's rights and feelings with such little thought or compassion. With a flash of insight, she realised that David's professed love was shallow and selfish, concerned only with taking and neglecting to give—it could not be compared with the love which Andrew knew for her which was all-encompassing and generous in every way. Yet she had treated Andrew's love lightly and blinded herself to the defects in David's character, dazzled by his looks and charm and personality and failing to penetrate deeply into his real nature, too infatuated to realise that David's first consideration would always be himself!

She reproached herself for planning, even briefly, to ask for her freedom in order to marry David or not, as *he* decided. She would have been placing herself in exactly the same position as before: more than that, she would have hurt Andrew who patiently waited for her to shake off a stupid, youthful infatuation; too, she would be hurting herself for she would lose so much that she now realised meant a great deal to her. Her marriage might have been the result of a hasty decision, an impulse, yet it was proving to be the wisest and most sensible step she had ever taken. She and Andrew were building something rare and precious on an excellent foundation—a happy marriage which would always be successful. She did not want to destroy the contentment and harmony which they shared. Only too vividly, she realised that her instinctive rejection of David's suggestion was due to a growing love for her husband—a new love which would be far greater and richer than the immature, selfish love she had given to David . . .

She was terribly afraid that it was too late, that she had hurt Andrew too deeply for forgiveness, that he would never understand that only through the humiliation of her guilt had she discovered the truth about her emotions. He would not believe that she was free of David at last —that she was on the verge of loving him as he deserved to be loved, as he wanted to be loved and as he hoped she would one day love him. She said his name tentatively, stubbing her cigarette.

He turned to look at her briefly and his eyes were cold, stark with pain and disappointment. But she searched in vain for a hint of anger and she took new hope. "Well, Sarah?"

There seemed to be nothing to say. There were no excuses she could offer. She had met David without her husband's knowledge. She had accepted his kisses and welcomed his embrace without a thought for the loyalty she owed to Andrew. It was pointless to pretend that her meeting with David had been the innocent encounter of mere friends for Andrew knew her too well, had always been able to see through any subterfuge on her part, piercing the veil of lies and deceit without difficulty.

She shook her head. Tears sprang to her eyes and she turned away so that he should not see them for she still had some vestige of pride.

Andrew's mouth twisted bitterly. He was not angry. He was merely disillusioned and desperately hurt by her behaviour. Impulsively, he had decided to drive to London, believing that there had been a hint of loneliness in her voice, a faint need of him, when they had spoken together on the telephone. He had realised that he would miss her terribly during the few days she was away and suddenly determined that there was nothing to keep him in Avering when he could be with his wife. It had been a cruel blow to his love for her to discover that she had wasted no time in contacting the man she undoubtedly still loved and wanted. It emphasised to him that he had failed in his attempts to make her happy during the last three months. Their marriage was far from being the success he had believed it to be—and he did not know if she was an accomplished actress or if he had managed to deceive himself because he desired so much of their life together. There was little point in continuing the farce now. It would be futile to keep her bound by their agreement—an arrangement which seemed to him more than ridiculous now. Her dishevelled appearance had told its own story. He had interrupted a lover's interlude—and he was bitter when he thought of his patience, his conviction born of love that one day she would be willing to accept him as a husband in every sense of the word, that he only had to give her enough time and she would grow out of her love for David Montrose. How wrong he had been! How easily he had been deceived! Whatever fascination the man possessed for Sarah, it was obvious that it was as strong as ever—therefore the only solution was to make an end to the farce of their marriage as soon as possible.

He had been afraid to speak during that long silence, hoping against hope that she would give him an explanation he could accept, willing to go more than halfway to believe whatever she told him, prepared to discount the evidence of his own eyes and the knowledge of his heart. But he had waited in vain—and now, as she turned away from him, he realised only too clearly that she had no explanation to offer, that she was guilty of at least the intention of being unfaithful if he had arrived in time to prevent the deed. He scarcely blamed Montrose. He was the type of man who would accept any opportunity which came his way where women were concerned—and he could believe that Sarah had thrown herself at his head. He fully believed that it had been Sarah who contacted the man and he did not need to look far for her motives. She was still in love with him—that was undeniable.

He forced himself to speak coldly despite the longing he knew to take her in his arms and impress upon her how much he loved her and how empty his life would be without her. "I'm glad that you find it impossible to lie to me, Sarah," he said. "I think we both understand that there's only one explanation for your behaviour—and I understand your reluctance to make that explanation."

"You're leaping to conclusions!" she retorted, lifting her chin defiantly—a defiance born of pain.

Again that bitter smile twisted his lips. "I don't think so. It doesn't take much stretching of my imagination to know why Montrose was here with you—and if you doubt it, then take a look at yourself in a mirror."

Her hands went instinctively to her hair and her mouth—and then she flushed. "Nothing happened," she said slowly.

He raised an eyebrow. "You're the only one who knows the truth of that statement, Sarah—except for Montrose, of course, and I've no intention of asking him to confirm it."

She stared at him. "You don't believe me?"

He shrugged. "I'm not interested enough to wonder about it, my dear. Whatever happened between you and David Montrose is a matter for your own conscience—I don't want to listen to any details."

"I've never known you like this, Andrew," she said slowly, wonderingly. "You're like a stranger."

He crossed to the decanters and helped himself to another drink. "You *are* a stranger, Sarah—I didn't think you were capable of being underhand but it proves how little I really know about you."

The indifference of his tone stung her and she went to him impulsively, laying her hand on his arm. "Don't be so cold-blooded, Andrew. Why can't you lose your temper—or behave like any other husband would?"

He looked down at her. "It doesn't occur to you that I may not feel like any other husband, does it? You don't seem to realise that I'm unaffected by your behaviour because it doesn't bother me unduly. After all, I've no real claim on you, Sarah. You've never pretended to love me and I've never asked anything of you but your friendship—so I don't lose anything. I've never had it to lose, my dear. If I'm reacting like a friend who hates to see you making a fool of yourself yet is in no position to prevent it, then it isn't so surprising, is it? I could almost say that it really isn't my business what you do—I'm only a friend to you. You can always rely on my friendship, of course."

Her eyes filled with astonishment. "But you love me, Andrew. You do love me, don't you?" It was so very important that he should still love her. Without his love, her life would be barren and bleak and she would have lost something infinitely valuable.

"Does it make any difference?" he asked wryly.

Sarah was hurt and bewildered. "Of course it does!" she exclaimed.

He shook his head. "You met Montrose because you wanted to do so. Despite everything, you're still in love with him. How can it matter to you whether or not

I love you? Surely the only important thing is whether or not Montrose is in love with you?"

"Oh, he says so," she replied absently.

He bit his lip against the pain which her words brought. "I see," he said slowly. "What happens now, Sarah?"

"That's up to you, isn't it?"

"I've no intention of holding you to our agreement," he assured her after a momentary pause. "I shall take steps to have our marriage annulled."

The finality in his voice left her with a feeling of stunned incredulity. With all her heart, she longed to tell him that she wanted their marriage to continue, that she wanted to spend the rest of her life making him happy—atoning for the hurt and humiliation she had caused him, that David no longer meant anything to her, that she needed Andrew and his love now more than ever. But the words were stilled by the blank inscrutability of his expression and her realisation that she had discovered the truth too late. Her heart sank. Slowly, his love had been dying for want of encouragement, for lack of hope, and now he no longer loved her. She did not need to hear the truth from him—the lack of warmth in his eyes and manner, the calm acceptance of her default, his ready decision to end their marriage—all these things emphasised only too cleariy that he had ceased to love her and she had no choice but to agree to the annulment . . .

11

FRANCES rummaged in her handbag for cigarettes and offered the case to Sarah who shook her head. She flicked her lighter into flame and applied it to the cigarette she placed between her lips. Then, slowly, she exhaled the blue-grey smoke, her eyes thoughtful as she watched her cousin's restless pacing and noticed the tightly clenched hands.

"It sounds rather unreasonable of Andrew," she said quietly. "I know he was furious to find David here—and I can understand that, remembering that you were very fond of David once—but it really doesn't sound concrete enough reason to end your marriage. Frankly, I'm staggered. I thought you and Andrew were so happy."

Sarah shrugged. "It was a mistake from the beginning," she said and her voice was hard with the effort to prevent any emotion breaking through. "I should never have married Andrew." She hesitated to add: *"in the circumstances"* but it was in her mind. Had she given herself time to get over David and realise that she had always instinctively loved Andrew, then a marriage between them would have been a success. But to marry him simply because she was bitter and lonely had been a terrible mistake, wronging Andrew far more than herself. Briefly she wondered if Frances had believed them to be happily married. It would imply that outwardly at least they had managed to deceive family and friends even if they were unable to pretend to themselves that all was well.

"I'm very sorry, Sarah," Frances said gently and she was sincere. Despite her own disappointment, she had really hoped that Andrew would find happiness with Sarah and believing that he had done so, she had been able to forget the hopes she had entertained where he was concerned and concentrate on the new love which David had evoked in her heart.

Sarah turned to flash a warm smile at her cousin. "Thank you. I'm sorry too—but I suppose there's nothing to do but accept the situation and think about making a new life for myself."

A stab of fear pierced Frances and she looked up swiftly. "With David?"

"I don't know." The reply was curt. She moved towards the telephone. "Would you like some coffee? I can telephone to Room Service."

Frances glanced at her watch. "I wish I had the time but I've arranged to meet a friend for coffee, Sarah. I suppose you'll be staying in Town for the time being?"

"Yes. Not here, though. I shall probably go to the flat."

"You could come home," Frances suggested quietly.

"No!" The exclamation was sharp. Hastily, Sarah went on: "I don't think I can face being questioned by everyone just yet. I know they'll be kind and sympathetic but at the same time they'll want to know just why Andrew and I have broken up and I don't feel like making explanations."

"Is it only David?"

Sarah turned to look at her cousin, struck by the tone of her voice. "You're fond of David, aren't you?" she asked slowly.

Frances forced a smile. "We're good

friends. I think he's very nice." She kept her tone light, unaware of what lay behind Sarah's unexpected question.

"Would you marry him if it were possible?"

"It isn't likely that he'll ever ask me to marry him," Frances protested, evading a direct reply. "I told you—we're just friends."

"But if he did?" Sarah insisted.

Frances stubbed her cigarette and rose to her feet, gathering up her gloves and handbag. "That's a very difficult question to answer, Sarah. Now I really must go or I shall be late." She smiled. "Don't worry too much—Andrew's too fond of you to let you go without a fight, you know. He's angry and hurt now, of course, but I'm sure he'd be willing to try again if you asked him."

"I wouldn't think of asking him to do so," Sarah said sharply.

"It's your life," Frances said with a little sigh. She moved towards the door. "I'll telephone you later, Sarah—perhaps we could have lunch together tomorrow?"

Sarah nodded. "All right. When are you going back to Avering?"

"Tomorrow evening, I think. Why?"

"I suppose I must get in touch with the parents and tell them—unless Andrew has already done so, of course. They're bound to be shocked and disappointed. I shall have to break the news to them myself even if Andrew has spoken first—they'd think it so odd if they didn't hear from me."

"What are you going to tell them?"

"The truth. That Andrew and I have parted and that our marriage will be annulled." She raised her chin proudly. "That I shall stay in London for a while until the comments have died down. They'll understand that I don't want to run the risk of seeing too much of Andrew."

Frances kissed her cousin's cheek briefly and took her departure. As she made her way to her appointment, she was very thoughtful, wondering what had actually happened between Sarah and David on the previous day, wishing she knew the full story of Andrew's decision to end his marriage to her cousin. Did David already know the news? Had Sarah already been in touch with him? Supposing she had been mistaken about David: he might still love Sarah, after all. There had to be a reason for his swift response to her telephone call and his eagerness to meet her again. It was only too possible that he had urged Sarah to make an end to her marriage because of their mutual love. Seated in the taxi which drove her through the busy thoroughfares of the city, she leaned against the cool leather and stared unseeingly at the passing traffic, the throng of pedestrians and the gaily-decorated shop windows. She had no claim on David. Her love was no justification for possessiveness. He was free to do as he pleased and to follow his inclination. For all she knew, he might well be amusing himself with her temporarily only so that he could learn if Sarah was happy, if she was well and what her movements were. She disliked the suspicion which stole through her at this thought but she could not dismiss it lightly —and she could not deny that he had been with Sarah on the previous day. Sarah had looked guilty and her appearance had been far from immaculate—the tense atmosphere alone had been evidence that they were caught out in a clandestine meeting.

She had been hurt and fearful but she had been careful to give no sign of her feelings, to display no curiosity regarding his presence in Sarah's hotel suite, when he drove her to the house where she was staying with friends. She had sensed that he appreciated her tact but at the same time he must have been vaguely puzzled by her apparent indifference to his actions.

She stepped from the taxi and paid off the driver. Then she turned towards the restaurant as David stepped swiftly forward to greet her, a smile curving his lips, a hint of warm admiration touching his blue eyes. Her smile was friendly but not effusive: she had swiftly discovered that he was intrigued by her air of reserve and lack of eagerness to be with him. She had even more reason now to safeguard against his awareness of the depth of her feeling for him.

David looked down at her, small, slight and oddly attractive with her piquant good looks. Despite the air of appealing fragility which she possessed, he knew that she was a very capable young woman with a mind of her own and a direct approach. He admired her poise and coolness, her unreserved honesty. At the same time, he was a little piqued that she failed to respond to the warmth of his attentions yet pleased that she still remained something of an enigma to him. They had met frequently during the last few months and fallen into an easy familiarity and he enjoyed her company. He always felt stimulated to further efforts by her lack of response to his personable charm.

"Punctual as ever!" he commended.

She preceded him into the restaurant and they sat down at a table. A waitress hurried to take his order and when she had left them, she replied: "I thought I might be late. I've just come from the Gower Hotel."

He raised an eyebrow. "Paying a call on Sarah and her husband?"

"Sarah. Andrew has gone back to Avering," she said calmly.

"That was a brief visit. I hope I didn't provoke a disagreement between them," he said lightly, taking out his cigarette case.

Frances shook her head to his offer of a cigarette and watched him as he busied himself with his lighter. "I don't know

198

what happened," she told him slowly, "but it seems that they've decided to break up."

His movements were stilled—but only for a moment, then he continued to light his cigarette. "That's rather interesting," he commented.

"You don't seem very surprised."

He smiled at her. "I'm not. I've never believed that Sarah could be happy with Whitaker. For one thing, she was in too much of a hurry to marry him. For another . . ."

"She married him on the rebound from you?" Frances finished for him.

He shrugged. "It's possible, isn't it?"

"Oh, it's possible—if one assumes that she was in love with you, David."

"I never had any doubts on that score," he told her with an almost insolent confidence.

Coffee was brought at that moment and Frances occupied herself with adding sugar and stirring the hot, fragrant liquid. "You're always very sure of yourself where women are concerned, aren't you?" she asked and she deliberately introduced a teasing note into her question.

His eyes were warmly-provocative. "As a rule." Once again, he found it difficult to reconcile her relationship to Sarah. They were totally different in character and temperament. Perhaps it was for this reason that he continued his friendship with Frances Kendrick. She had a definite appeal for him but he had never bothered to analyse his interest too closely. "Occasionally I meet a woman who manages to keep me guessing," he added.

"Did Sarah come into that category?"

"Perhaps." His reply was non-committal. He relaxed in his seat and regarded her thoughtfully. "So Sarah has left Andrew Whitaker? Do you think there will be a divorce?"

Frances shrugged. "I imagine so. Of course, it may be just a slight disagreement exaggerated by them both, I can't see Andrew giving Sarah up so easily."

David pursed his lips. "I admit that I received a similar impression. Whitaker strikes me as being the type of man to hold on to his possessions—and I can't say I'd blame him if he decided to wait a while and hope that Sarah will go back to him.

She's a very beautiful woman and any man would be proud to have her as his wife."

"Any man?" Frances queried. "Including you?"

He knocked grey ash from his cigarette with a nonchalant gesture. "That's an odd question, Frances."

"Surely you can answer it," she returned swiftly. "After all, it isn't very long since you admitted to me that you were in love with Sarah. It's a little late for pretence now."

"You were in love with Whitaker," he reminded her. "Still are, I suppose. You should be delighted that one day he'll be a free man. There's always the possibility that he might marry you—it's a chance, anyway, and most women know how to make the most of such chances."

A faint colour stained her cheeks. "There'll never be anyone for Andrew but Sarah. I knew that years ago. If she hadn't agreed to marry him, he would never have married at all—and if their marriage ends in divorce, it's highly unlikely that he'd ever look around for another wife."

He stretched out a hand to touch hers gently. "I'm sorry, Frances."

She moved her hand away from his touch with an abrupt movement—and then covered the instinctive action by lifting her coffee cup to her lips. "I don't need sympathy," she said lightly. "I wouldn't marry Andrew if it were possible to do so."

He searched her face with swift incredulity in his eyes. "Then you're no longer in love with him?"

"Not in the least."

"I'm delighted to hear it," he said warmly. "So you took my advice after all."

She wrinkled her forehead in a tiny frown. "Your advice?" she echoed.

His smile had a hint of tender indulgence. "Don't tell me you've forgotten! To forget that you ever cared for Whitaker and not waste your life hankering for him. I believe I also said something about finding happiness with another man but there's plenty of time for that."

Her brow cleared. "Yes, I remember, David." She looked at him sharply. "But you didn't take your own advice, did you? You're still in love with Sarah."

He raised an eyebrow. "You seem very sure about that." There was a brief silence as their eyes met for a long moment: enig-

202

matic, half-smiling blue eyes and clear, direct, almost accusing grey—in passing David thought how very grey her eyes were yet he had seen them soften with warm affection until they were almost blue. He looked down at the table, idly stirred his coffee. He wondered what had passed between Sarah and Frances Kendrick that morning: if Sarah had divulged the gist of her conversation with him on the previous day; if she had confided in her cousin that she was still in love with him and meant to marry him when she obtained her freedom. It was true that he had not been surprised by Frances' news although he had not expected such a sudden change in the circumstances. Twenty-four hours ago, Sarah had been adamant in her determination to remain with Whitaker until a year of marriage had expired—now she had left him and was apparently looking forward to her freedom with eager anticipation. Had she changed her mind and decided to risk her happiness with him, after all? Or had Whitaker finally decided that he could take no more of such an unsatisfactory marriage and issued the ultimatum that either Sarah returned with him to Avering on different terms or their marriage was at an end? David was consumed with curiosity. It was also curious that Sarah had not been in touch with him: if the decision had been hers, surely she would have wanted to tell him immediately that she was prepared to take him up on his suggestion.

He had been thinking things over during the night, cool clearheadedness taking the place of the ardent emotion which had been stirred in him by the thought of meeting Sarah again and by the actuality of her intoxicating beauty. For she was a beautiful woman and a very desirable one in his eyes. Yet he could not visualise a time when they would be man and wife—and he wondered if he shrank from the thought. Perhaps the emotion she stirred in him was not love. After all, he had managed to live without her. Certainly he had missed her very much but he had given himself little time to brood over what might have been if he had married her when she was so insistent that he should do so. He reminded himself firmly of the many times, both as a child and as a man, when he had refused something offered to him with the clear conviction that it did not interest or appeal to him only to want it desperately when it proved unattainable. It was a quirk of his character—an odd quirk but an undeniable one. It could apply so easily to his feelings for Sarah.

To him, marriage was a very serious undertaking and he had been wholy in earnest when he told Sarah that he would only marry her if they had proved their ability to live together in happiness. Knowing himself so well and remembering so vividly the many times he had been moved by the impulse to ask Sarah to marry him only to draw back at the last moment because of a strange conviction that their destinies did not lie together, he had no intention of committing himself to such a deliberate and serious step until he was really sure that it was the right one to take.

Recalling Sarah's instinctive refusal to hurt the man she had married, it was only logical to suppose that her emotions were confused, that she was no longer as sure of her love for him as she professed to be, that there was every likelihood that she was content in her marriage and more than halfway to being in love with Andrew Whitaker. This idea had not pained him as much as it surely should have done if he was in love with her. He had been disappointed, of course, but perhaps his pride had suffered rather than his heart. He had been spoiled by women and it was a rare thing for him to know rejection or refusal.

It had been interesting to study the reaction of Andrew Whitaker to his presence in Sarah's hotel suite. He had been compelled to admire the man's restraint and forced to admit that he was undoubtedly very much in love with Sarah. David was a swift and clever judge of character and, despite the natural animosity of two men who desired the same women, he had known an instinctive liking and admiration for Andrew Whitaker and a deep-rooted conviction that Sarah had married the one man who could make her really happy although she might not fully realise the fact at the moment.

He pulled his thoughts back to the present and glanced up from the contemplation of his coffee cup to smile at Frances. "What has Sarah been telling you?" he asked lightly.

Frances was taken aback by the direct question. "Nothing at all—if you're referring to whatever took place between you and Sarah yesterday."

"You're quick to assume that something happened."

She picked up the lighter that lay on the table and toyed with it restlessly. He placed his hand over hers and stilled the unquiet movements.

"Frances—I'm going to be completely frank with you," he said slowly. "Please listen to what I have to say without interruption—then you may comment." Concisely, unemotionally, he told her of his suggestion to Sarah and her reactions: he told her of his fear that he had been too hasty, that it seemed likely that he was to blame for the break-up of Sarah's marriage and that he very much regretted it; he told her that he no longer loved Sarah and had no wish either to live with her or to marry her. He finished the long recital with the wry words: "Now what do I do? Supposing Sarah left Whitaker in order to accept my offer—how do I tell her that I've changed my mind?"

Frances had listened carefully to all he said. She displayed no surprise or emotion or disgust, keeping a tight rein on the chaotic feelings which swept through her. It seemed incredible that David could have been so foolish yet she had no choice but to believe him. She pushed away the cold remains of her coffee and faced him squarely as the echo of his question died away. She refrained from commenting on the stupidity of his actions. Instead, she said quietly: "I suggest you tell Sarah the truth. She isn't a child, you know—she's well able to face facts. If she is still in love with you, then she has the right to know exactly what your feelings are, David."

There was a faint gleam of gratitude in his eyes as he regarded her thoughtfully. "It's a damn awkward position to be in, though—oh, I know it's all my own fault and I can't imagine now what on earth possessed me! I'm not usually the impulsive type. You do believe me, Frances—I really don't care for Sarah any more."

"I've known that for a long time," she returned coolly.

His eyes narrowed—then he smiled involuntarily. "What a shrewd person you are—and how deep! I sometimes wonder if I shall ever know the real Frances Kendrick. I can't think of any other woman of my acquaintance who would have taken all this so calmly."

She smiled faintly. "I appreciate your confidence, David, and I understand your difficulty. But at the same time, I'm not affected by the position, so of course I've taken it calmly." The lie came easily to her.

He nodded, accepting her words at their face value. A mad impulse suddenly leaped in him as their eyes met across the table and words sprang to his lips. With an effort, he fought them back and tried to suppress the fleeting impulse but the idea strengthened with the passing moments . . .

Frances was puzzled by the strange light in his eyes, by the evident intention to speak and the obvious hesitation, and she wondered what was in his thoughts.

As though he sensed her bewilderment, he said with a laugh: "I'm on the point of rushing in again where angels fear to tread.

You'll think I'm quite mad, Frances—but I've just realised how much I want to marry you." He took her hand and pressed her slim fingers warmly, his eyes resting on her face for a brief moment with tenderness in their depths. "It isn't Sarah at all—it's you, my dear."

She caught her breath, her eyes wide with astonishment. Then the sheer idiocy of the situation caught at her sense of humour and she began to laugh. For a moment, he was hurt—then he too saw the funny side of his proposal and joined in her laughter. "Oh, David!" she gasped when she could speak. "You idiot!" The word was an endearment. "You'll know what you do want one day!"

He was abruptly serious. "I want you, Frances. Will you marry me?" He leaned forward, tense, waiting for her reply.

"Oh, why not?" she said lightly. "Yes, I'll marry you—but I think I'm as mad as you to accept!"

He grinned at her boyishly. "We'll be mad together—but happy! I *know* we'll be happy, Frances."

12

THE rest of the day passed in a feverish whirl. David telephoned his chambers and cancelled all his appointments. Then, hand in hand like a pair of children, they strolled along the busy thoroughfares of the great metropolis, talking little but content to be together, eagerly surveying the contents of jewellers' windows in quest of an engagement ring, David determined that only the best was good enough for the woman he was going to marry. It was a sunny day and the streets were crowded with girls in gay dresses and young men in holiday mood. But David and Frances were oblivious to everyone but their two selves, caught up in the excitement and incredulous wonder of a shared future.

Frances allowed him to sweep her off her feet, to plan for the future, to thrill her with exciting suggestions of a honeymoon abroad and a country house, to over-rule her qualms so that she readily agreed to marry him within a few days. Her calm composure had been shattered for the first time since he met her and David was delighted to discover the warm eagerness, the gaiety and the sweetness of her true nature.

They reached the cool precincts of St. James' Park, their feet having led them unknowingly in that direction, and they seated themselves on the grass, relaxing comfortably. David brought out his cigarettes and lighter and they were silent for a few minutes, surveying the attractive scene before them, watching the small family groups around them and the occasional pair of lovers strolling along the paths, aware yet not aware of the traffic which streamed along the Mall in the background, listening to the birds in the trees above their heads and the faint murmur of activity about them.

David rolled over on to his back and lay looking up at the cloudless sky. Frances looked down at him, smiling. It was incredible that she was actually going to marry him. It had all happened so swiftly, so unexpectedly—and she did not for a moment regret her acceptance of his strange proposal. He had not mentioned his feelings for her but it was not necessary. The song in her heart was sufficient. He loved her—she knew it and there was no room for doubt, no need for words. The silent communion between them was ample proof of mutual love, of the need to be together for the rest of their lives, of the happiness which lay in store for them.

She tickled his cheek with a strand of long grass and he grinned at her. "Happy?"

She nodded. "Very."

He caught the hand which held the blade of grass and carried the slim fingers to his lips. His eyes met hers and she was suddenly shy because of the ardency of his gaze.

"Love me?" he asked.

Frances nodded. This was no time for pretence. She need never again hide behind her natural reserve, guard against the revelation of her love for him. "Yes, David."

"I can't believe it's true," he said and he sighed—a deep sigh which was tremulous with happiness. "I feel about sixteen," he added lightly. "Why didn't I realise before that you were the one I wanted, Frances? Why was I so blind?" He did not wait for an answer. "I've swept you off your feet, haven't I? You do mean to marry me? You won't suddenly change your mind?"

She leaned over him and touched his mouth briefly with her own. She sensed the sudden tensing of his body, knew the quivering response of his lips and felt his arm tighten abruptly about her slim waist. "As long as you're sure, David," she said against his lips, a terrifying fear leaping within her.

He sat up abruptly, drew her closer to him. "I've been all kinds of a fool, darling —but I know what I want now. I can't wait to marry you. I'm so terribly afraid that I shall lose you—that something will happen to make you change your mind or prevent us getting married. I've always been frank with you, Frances. You know that I've believed myself in love before. I swear to you that I've never felt like this before for any woman. Love and marriage have never been compatible in my eyes, before—but I can't imagine loving you and not wanting to marry you."

His voice rang with such inherent sincerity that abruptly her eyes filled with tears. Unashamed of her emotion, she lifted a hand to dash the tears from her lashes and gave a little laugh. "I'm crying because I'm so happy, David—no other reason. It's a failing where women are concerned."

Tenderly he kissed the wet cheeks and brushed her lashes with his lips, oblivious to the interested gaze of those who passed by. "I didn't know you loved me," he said. "I asked you to marry me but I didn't think I stood an earthly chance of success. You were always so cool, so untouchable—and now I find that you're so very warm and sweet and utterly adorable." He sought her mouth and kissed her briefly but ardently.

Frances released herself and flushed as she met the frankly curious gaze of two children who stood two or three yards away, watching them. "David—let's walk on," she said. "This is a public park, after all."

He grinned. "I've never kissed a woman

in a public park before, to my recollection. Certainly not in broad daylight. No one would believe that I'm a respectable lawyer. You've a bad influence on me, woman. I've ditched two important clients —drunk champagne in the middle of the day—and now, I've surrendered to the temptation to kiss you in a public park under the innocent gaze of young children!" He stood up and gave her his hands to help her to her feet. For a moment they faced each other, smiling. "I love you!" he said and his voice was happily triumphant.

She brushed her skirt and gathered up her bag and gloves. Then, hand in hand once more, they walked over the grass to the Mall and strolled down the wide, tree-lined avenue towards Trafalgar Square, totally unaware that everything about them—the way they walked, the linked hands, the exchanged smiles and tender glances—proclaimed to the world that they were in love . . .

By the fountains of Trafalgar Square, they paused to feed the pigeons, delighting in the favourite pastime of tourists, submitting to the persuasions of a photographer and laughing up at each other at their enjoyment of such simple things. Suddenly, Frances sobered—and David was so attuned to her mood that his hand tightened on her elbow and he guided her to a vacant seat nearby.

"What is it?" he asked anxiously. "What's wrong, Frances?"

She turned to him. "How on earth are we going to tell Sarah?"

A shadow flitted across his eyes. "Yes, it is going to be difficult," he replied slowly.

"It seems so natural to us, David—everything's just fallen into place. But only yesterday you asked Sarah to leave Andrew and live with you—and today you're engaged to me!"

He nodded. "I know. Things have happened with amazing swiftness. Yesterday I was a blind fool—today I'm the happiest man in London. But Sarah won't believe that—and she'll have to know sooner or later that I'm going to marry you." He smiled at her reassuringly. "Let's cross that bridge when we come to it. Frances."

"That's the easy way out," she demurred.

He spread his hands in a helpless

gesture. "Then what do you want to do? Go to Sarah now and tell her? Surely we can have this one day to ourselves, darling —with nothing to spoil it?"

"We'll have the rest of our lives," she reminded him. "And Sarah has nothing now—not you or Andrew."

He pursed his lips thoughtfully. "You think that Sarah has left Andrew because of me, don't you?"

"I don't know what to think," she replied honestly. "I know that she loved you very much—that she was still in love with you when she married Andrew. If she has left him because of you, David, then you've done a terrible thing."

His expression darkened. "Reproaches, Frances?"

"I'm sorry, David," she said quickly.

There was something in her tone that caused him to glance at her sharply. "What's on your mind?"

She hesitated. Then she said: "In all fairness to Sarah—and ourselves—I don't think we should announce our engagement or make any plans for getting married until we know what Sarah means to do."

He stared at her in astonishment. "You can't mean that!"

"Yes, I do," she told him firmly.

He laughed—a short, sharp laugh that held no amusement. "Supposing Sarah decides she wants to live with me—I hope you're not suggesting that you'd fade discreetly out of my life so that she can do so! Darling, you're voicing utter rubbish!"

"Please—listen to me, David," she pleaded gently. "We can't spring our news on Sarah without any warning. Why, she hasn't any idea how we feel about each other—she must believe that you're still in love with her. Without Andrew, she'll turn to you, confident that you'll be waiting for her. Can't you see that, darling? I know that's how I would feel, if I were in Sarah's position. But she might not care for you any more . . ."

"I wish that were true," he said earnestly, thinking of Sarah's passionate response to his kisses and her ardent declarations of love on the previous day.

Frances went on as though he had not interrupted her: ". . . and she'll tell you frankly that she's not interested in your proposal. It's even possible that she loves

Andrew now and they'll patch things up within a few days. But until we know, one way or the other, we can't make any plans."

He brought out his cigarettes, thrust one between his lips and ignited the flame of his lighter. He exhaled blue-grey cigarette smoke through his nostrils—the only indication of his disturbed thoughts. "We've already made our plans," he said with a hint of obstinacy in his tone.

"But they can be postponed for a little while," she pointed out.

"Agreed. But I want to marry you as soon as possible, Frances," he told her coolly.

She slipped her hand in his arm and tightened her fingers about his wrist. "I know—that's how I feel, David. But we have to consider Sarah's feelings. I'm so happy—and I want her to be happy too . . ."

"Not at our expense, surely?"

"Oh, darling, nothing can affect our happiness," she said gently. "We can afford to be generous. You used to be fond of Sarah—you were good friends. Could you marry me next week without feeling a little guilty about the way you've treated Sarah?"

Suddenly he smiled. "Appealing to my better nature? Honestly, darling, I don't see what good it will do to wait—and I can't see how we can help Sarah in any way—but I'll bow to your superior judgment in the matter. At least, it won't be very long before we find out what Sarah intends to do."

"I'm lunching with her tomorrow," Frances told him. "Perhaps she'll talk to me about her plans."

He nodded. "I expect she's wondering why I haven't been in touch with her— but I'm not supposed to know that her husband went back to Avering so abruptly." He glanced down at Frances as a thought struck him. "Didn't you tell Sarah that you were meeting me this morning?"

She shook her head. "No. I told her I was having coffee with a friend." She added: "She didn't seem curious."

"I'm not surprised. You have a natural reticence which prevents people from asking too many questions." He grinned. "It's taken me three months to break through that barrier but I was always determined to do so one day. I knew you couldn't be as much of an ice maiden as you seemed!"

Her expression was warmly loving. "If only you knew how difficult it was not to betray my real feelings, David. I fell in love with you very quickly, you know."

He smiled at her warmly, tenderly. "You keep your secrets well, my sweet. I used to pride myself on having an instinct in such matters but it shows how wrong one can be!" He threw his cigarette to the ground and crushed it to extinction with his heel. "You've never seen my flat, have you?" he went on. "It will be our home when we are married—until we find just the house we want—so it would be a good idea if you had a look round the place. It won't be very tidy. I'm not the tidy type, I'm afraid. But there's certain to be some food in the place and perhaps we can fix a snack meal this evening, unless you want to dine out somewhere."

She shook her head and the glance she gave him held a hint of provocation. "It will be nice to have you all to myself for a few hours, David—and I've no objection to being kissed as long as you can assure me that we won't have an audience."

He laughed and rose to his feet. "There'll be no audience, darling." He caught her hands and pulled her up and they walked together across the square, merging with the crowd and yet distinct from them by reason of their transparent happiness . . .

When she was eventually alone, much later that evening, Frances thought over the tumultuous events of the day and her heart was still singing with the joyous realisation of her hope that David might return her love one day. That day had come so much more quickly than she had dreamed possible. They were fortunate in that there were no obstacles to be overcome before they could marry. A short postponement was a mere trifle—and might not be necessary if Sarah patched up her rift with Andrew.

Frances had been surprised when David gave in so readily to her insistence that they should keep secret their engagement for the time being. She had never thought of him as being a malleable man yet at the same time she knew that he was always reasonable and understanding. He was naturally reluctant to postpone their marriage indefinitely and she was equally as impatient to be his wife but it was not compatible with her character to think of her own happiness and not give a thought to her cousin's present disappointment and pain which seemed to be all that she had attained in her marriage.

She was fully convinced that David was the only man who could make her happy and she had no doubts that he loved her —if there had been any lingering doubts, he would have swiftly dispelled them by his sweetness, consideration and warm tenderness that evening. A tiny smile touched her lips as she brushed her hair before the mirror of her dressing-table—a smile that was warmly reminiscent of the happiness she had experienced with David until a brief while ago when they had reluctantly parted on the steps of her friends' house.

She gazed at her reflection. Had her friends noticed the stars in her eyes, the colour in her cheeks and the tremulousness of her lips, the effort to be apparently composed as she answered their questions on the manner in which she had spent her day? It had seemed an eternity before she could escape their kindly interest, bid them goodnight and slip up to her room. She tried to view herself dispassionately and then she knew that the truth was written all over her—she was a woman in love content in the knowledge that her love was returned. She wondered if it would be as apparent to Sarah on the following day or if she would find it possible to keep the truth from her cousin.

She sat before the dressing-table for a long time, twining the long strands of her chestnut-coloured hair about her fingers and brushing them to satin smoothness while she indulged in roseate dreams of her future with David, oblivious to the lateness of the hour and happier than she had ever been in her life before. She could not possibly doubt the joy which lay in store for her as David's wife.

But the situation could prove to be awkward and she did not relish the task of telling Sarah the news—particularly now when her cousin was smarting from the humiliation of her break with Andrew and debating the proposal which David had so foolishly and thoughtlessly put forward. Frances could not imagine that Sarah would seriously consider taking such a step—but she did not *know* and therein lay the danger. Naturally David would not hesitate to point out to Sarah that the circumstances had changed but Frances did not wish the question to arise. She did not think badly of David for making that proposal. Oddly enough, to her it was a clarifying symbol. She was confident that if David had really been in love with Sarah, either now or previously, he could not have made such a suggestion. She thought of his undoubted eagerness to marry her and that was proof enough for Frances of the sincerity of his love. She knew that where she was concerned such an arrangement would not enter his head nor would he welcome it if she were to reason that they should discover before marriage if they could live together amicably and find happiness. It had to be marriage or nothing and so he had proved to her satisfaction only that evening. For he was an idealist at heart and now that he had found his ideal, he could not treat their mutual love lightly. He was a man capable of loving only once and now that love had touched his life and his heart with such intensity of emotion his only thought was to marry the woman who had inspired it.

Frances could dismiss the light affairs of his past without a qualm, placing as little importance on them as she knew he did where her once-admitted love for Andrew was concerned. She felt no jealousy or curiosity—only a deep certainty that now and in the future she would be the only woman in David's life.

13

SARAH slowly pulled on the long, tan gloves which completed her ensemble and threw one last glance at the silent telephone before she left her suite and closed the door with a sharp little sound. All morning she had lived with the hope that Andrew might telephone or arrive unexpectedly at the hotel. Surely he would change his mind and decide to give their marriage another chance! It could not be true that after so many years of unswerving loyalty, his love had finally ceased to be! She could not imagine a future without Andrew and she felt that life would hold no happiness for her if it did not contain the man she had married and whose love she had disdained until it was too late. But she had heard nothing from him and she was forced to the realisation that the happiness she had known with him had come to an end. For the first time in her life, she felt completely alone —and she did not like the feeling.

She stepped out of the lift and crossed the thickly-carpeted foyer of the hotel. Her beauty and her elegance caused several heads to turn as she moved gracefully towards the swing doors but she was indifferent to their admiration. She did not notice the man who had just entered the hotel and stood watching her progress towards him.

David thought he had never seen her look so beautiful and decided that it was the slight pallor which gave her that ethereal air. He detected a hint of sadness in her lovely eyes but he noticed the proud tilt of her chin and his eyes were warm with admiration.

He stepped forward to intercept her. "Sarah."

She stopped abruptly. "Oh, David." She said his name absently as though he were a casual acquaintance whose unexpected appearance caused no surprise or interest.

"I'm glad I caught you," he said. 'You're on your way to meet Frances, I presume."

"Yes—I'm having lunch with her," she told him.

"You've time to have a quick drink with me," he said and took her by the elbow. Before she could protest, he had guided her towards the Cocktail Lounge in his usual masterful manner.

She looked up at him and remembered the circumstances of their last meeting. A faint colour stained her cheeks. It was amazing that only two days ago she had been convinced that her happiness was with him and no one else in the world— and that now she could view him without a stir of emotion other than embarrassment. It seemed incredible that she had ever believed herself to be in love with him: he was attractive and personable, it was true, but he completely lacked the qualities which she loved in Andrew. It was unnecessary to make comparisons. She loved Andrew with every part of her being and she had always loved him as instinctively as though he were the true complement of herself. She had been foolish and blind for so many years, looking beyond him for her happiness, unable to understand or perceive that all she wanted in life was so close at hand. And now, when she did understand and realise the truth, it was too late—Andrew no longer loved her or wanted her as his wife. Her feeling for David had been nothing but a youthful, heady emotion which did not plumb the true depths of her being. Now she could be grateful that he had proved reluctant to marry her for she knew that she would never have been so happy with him as she had been with Andrew in the last few months.

"I've only a few minutes to spare, David," she said.

"Long enough," he assured her. He swiftly procured drinks and they sat down at a nearby table. "I want to talk to you about Frances," he said without further preliminary.

She threw him a swift, probing glance, surprised by the unusual seriousness of his tone and the quiet intensity of his manner. "Frances? Is she all right?" she asked with the urgency of sudden dread, wondering if he had brought bad news.

"She was fine when I saw her yesterday," he assured her. He hesitated briefly and then went on, his eyes meeting hers with frank, unashamed appeal for understanding in their depths. "I came to tell you that Frances and I are going to be married, Sarah."

"You're going to marry Frances?" she echoed, stunned by his statement. It took her a moment or two to make any sense of his news—then she was incredulous.

He brought out his cigarette case and flicked it open. "It must be a shock to you," he said slowly. "I still can't believe it myself—but I do know it's true."

She bent her head over the flame of his lighter and drew on the cigarette she had taken from his case. "I'm afraid I'm completely at a loss, David. Supposing you start again. Did I really hear you say that you're going to marry Frances?"

He smiled briefly. "That's right."

"But only two days ago you were urging me to leave Andrew and live with you, David," she reminded him. "Or was that all a dream?"

"It wasn't a dream," he assured her. "Frances tells me that you and your husband *have* parted, Sarah—if I'm to blame for that, then I'm deeply sorry. Look here, it's pointless to beat about the bush. I'm not in love with you. I never have been. Seeing you again must have gone to my head but I've had time to think things over and I want you to know that I couldn't possibly marry you—ever! I love Frances and have every intention of marrying her as soon as possible."

"I see," Sarah said slowly. She no longer cared what David did with his life but a tiny vestige of remaining pride teased her in that moment with the reminder that he had never wanted to marry her—even while he had avowed his passionate love for her only two days ago. Yet he could declare his intention to marry Frances without delay and not display the faintest trace of embarrassment. She threw back her head and let a cloud of cigarette smoke drift from her nostrils. There was something faintly contemptuous in the gesture. She would not betray any sign of dismay or humiliation. "What a despicable person you are, David," she said without any trace of emotion in her voice.

His fingers beat a restless tattoo on the table top. "I must seem so to you," he admitted. "I can appreciate the way you feel, Sarah—but I couldn't allow you to go on thinking that I was ready to step into Whitaker's shoes now that you've left him.

233

My behaviour was despicable and I have no excuse—except that I imagined myself in love with you. But even that isn't sufficient reason for breaking up your marriage. What will you do now, Sarah? Is there any chance of patching things up with Whitaker—or is that unthinkable?"

She shrugged. "It would be very easy for me to let you take the blame, David—but I don't think you have any conscience so it wouldn't be troubled. My marriage didn't break up because of you. You knew its eccentric basis and its unsatisfactory circumstances. Well, Andrew's patience gave out—and that isn't very surprising, is it? He wishes to end our marriage—I don't. You see, I'm not in love with you, either, David. When you asked me if I'd fallen in love with my husband, you were very near the truth. I've always loved Andrew but I've only just realised it." Her eyes were pools of sadness but swiftly she pulled herself together and smiled at him bravely.

He placed his hand over hers and pressed it gently. "We've both been very foolish, Sarah. Are you quite sure that there isn't any chance of making something of your marriage, despite everything?"

"Quite sure," she said firmly, remembering the finality of Andrew's words and her own conviction that his love for her was dead for ever. A silence fell between them and neither knew quite how to break it. At last, she asked with interest: "When did you discover that it was Frances you wanted to marry?" He did not answer immediately and when she glanced at him she was surprised to note the merest trace of colour in his cheeks and a sheepishness in his expression.

"Yesterday," he admitted at last.

She nodded. "It happened very suddenly."

"Life's like that, isn't it?" He searched her eyes. "And you, Sarah? When did you find out that you were really in love with your husband? You seemed quite sure that I was the one you wanted the other day."

She smiled. "It was the same day—after you'd gone and I was alone with Andrew. I realised what a fool I'd been—that Andrew was worth three like you and that the best thing I'd ever done was to marry him. Then he told me that he wanted to have our marriage annulled." She sighed briefly.

"Perhaps it was rather a blow to his pride to find you with me," he suggested. "I don't think he believed our meeting was just a friendly get-together—in fact, I'm damn sure he knew it wasn't! It seems unlikely that he would put up with everything for three months and then decide to call the whole thing off just like that, Sarah. He was angry and hurt—and probably he's convinced that you want your freedom so he's doing the generous thing."

"I wish I could believe that," she said quietly. "But I know Andrew too well. I've hurt him too much—and now I can't hurt him any more. He no longer cares for me." Her voice was expressionless but the sadness in her eyes was unmistakable and compelling.

"I wish there was something I could do," David told her sincerely. "But I can't help feeling that I've done more than enough!"

"It isn't your fault," she said quickly. "I was a fool to telephone you in the first place, David. It was an impulse—and I should know better than to follow my impulses by now. I've made enough mistakes doing just that." Her tone was bitter.

"What happens now?"

She shrugged. "I don't know. Nothing. Andrew said he would attend to all the necessary arrangements. I'm not even sure what the annulment of a marriage entails."

He pursed his lips thoughtfully. "It's an unpleasant business. Sarah—more humiliating than divorce, in my opinion. There has to be full details given of your life together—and proof that you've never lived together as man and wife. I hate to think of you being mixed up in it."

"I haven't any choice," she reminded him.

He pulled thoughtfully at his lower lip. "Why not go down to Avering and see Whitaker? Tell him how you feel—ask him for another chance. I won't believe that your marriage is hopelessly sundered —not if you really love him and if he still cares anything for you."

"No!" she exclaimed swiftly, sharply. "That's out of the question!"

He looked at her keenly. "You have your fair share of pride too, Sarah—

perhaps too much. Surely your happiness is more important than the humbling of your pride?"

"You don't understand, David," she told him quietly. "Andrew would immediately think that you'd let me down again —certainly he wouldn't believe me if I told him that I was in love with him! It seems fantastic to *me* that I could be so blind for so long. Besides, I might be wrong. This feeling for Andrew might pass—perhaps I'm not really in love with anyone. Oh, I can't explain fully . . ."

"You're very confused," he said gently. "Maybe you're right. It might be wiser to give yourself a little time before you do anything—keep away from Andrew and try to sort out your emotions. Why don't you go abroad or visit some friends? It will take your husband some time to set the annulment proceedings in motion, I assure you—so if you did decide to see him and talk things over when you know what you really want, it wouldn't be too late."

"It's too late now," she said firmly. She glanced at her wristlet watch. "And I'm late for my appointment with Frances. I suppose she knows that you were coming to see me today?"

He shook his head. "I didn't tell her, Sarah. Frances wanted to keep our engagement secret for a while. She was thinking of your feelings and she impressed upon me that we should wait until we knew what your future plans were. But I didn't see the point of that. I decided it was only fair that you should know the exact circumstances."

Sarah's eyes narrowed. "Why should Frances be so considerate of my feelings? Surely you weren't such a fool as to tell her about us, David—about the ridiculous plans we were making for the future?"

"I've no secrets from Frances," he returned quietly.

"You had no right to divulge *my* secrets," she told him sharply, exasperatedly. "So, as far as she is aware, I'm still in love with you and I've left Andrew because of you—is that it?"

He nodded. "I expect that's the way Frances sees it, Sarah."

"Knowing that, she still agreed to marry you," Sarah pointed out.

He was slightly impatient as he retorted:

"Of course. Why not? She knows that I love her—she knows that I mean to marry her. Your break with Andrew is unfortunate and she's very upset about it—she's fond of you both, you know. But surely you wouldn't expect her to sacrifice her happiness and refuse to marry me because there was always the risk that you might want to take me up on a suggestion which I very much regret."

Suddenly Sarah began to laugh. "The whole situation is so ludicrous," she explained when she could speak coherently. "Honestly, I'd never believe it if it happened to anyone else—or if I read about it in a book! Surely these things don't really exist in real life? It's such a glorious mix-up—and somehow I can't see it being straightened out," she added soberly. "You and Frances will be all right but I can't see any future for myself or Andrew at the moment." She rose to her feet. "I must go—Frances will think something terrible has happened to me. Are you coming with me, David? Why not join us for lunch—a celebration lunch? I've no intention of pretending that I don't know of your engagement—and I want to drink to your happiness in the future. I think you will be happy, too. Frances is a very sweet person with her feet firmly on the ground and perhaps she'll stabilise you a little—at the same time, you'll be good for Frances. She's much too intense and reserved to really enjoy life."

He grinned. "That proves that you don't really know Frances," he said lightly. "She has a natural, spontaneous gaiety and a zest for living—and her reserve is carefully cultivated, I can assure you. She's afraid to show her feelings, that's the trouble—she's too sensitive. But I'll look after her in future," he added with determination.

They left the hotel and David hailed a taxi. It took them only a few minutes to reach the restaurant where Sarah had arranged to meet her cousin for lunch.

Frances was waiting in the foyer, sitting on a padded wall seat, anxiously scanning those who entered. She glanced up from her watch as Sarah and David came into the restaurant—and she was surprised to observe her cousin's companion. A swift stab of fear showed itself in her eyes as she rose slowly to her feet.

Sarah's smile of greeting was warm and affectionate. "Have you been waiting long?" she asked. "I'm sorry—but you must blame David. He talks too much."

David grinned at Frances and sought her hand which he squeezed reassuringly. "Hallo, darling. I hope you don't think that two's company and three's a crowd but Sarah has persuaded me to join you for lunch."

"I'm very pleased," Frances said slowly, bewildered. Sarah met her cousin's eyes levelly. "David's told me of your engagement—and I'm delighted. I insisted that we should have a celebration lunch."

"It will be our second," David put in lightly. "But probably not the last." He turned to Sarah. "Had you reserved a table?" When she nodded, he added: "I'll have a word with the head waiter and tell him to lay a third place. We can have a drink before we eat." He strode away from them.

Frances looked after him—and then turned to Sarah. "You must have been surprised when David told you that we were engaged," she said hesitantly. "It happened rather suddenly."

Sarah smiled. "So I gather. Don't look so worried, Frances—I've no objections. You're welcome to David and I hope you'll both be very happy."

The anxiety in Frances' expression cleared. "Then you're not in love with David?" she asked eagerly.

"Not in the least!" Sarah assured her swiftly.

"I thought—you see—David told me what happened between you the other day," Frances stumbled uncertainly.

"Yes, I know. We were both rather silly. But we've come to our senses now."

"Oh, I'm glad!" Frances exclaimed earnestly. "I've been feeling so guilty about promising to marry David. Then everything will be all right now—with you and Andrew, I mean?"

"I don't know," Sarah admitted. Her tone was cautious and deliberately light as she went on: "We'll have to wait and see what happens. I'm not going to do anything in a hurry—I've rushed in too often and made stupid mistakes."

"I think that's a sensible way of looking at it," Frances said firmly. "It wouldn't be fair to Andrew to go back to him unless you're really sure that you want to make something of your marriage."

Sarah was saved the necessity of making a reply as David returned to them with his swift, characteristic steps. She enjoyed the meal and for a brief hour or so was able to push the thoughts of Andrew to the back of her mind. David was in high good humour and kept them amused with anecdotes taken from his experiences in Court although Sarah noticed that he deliberately avoided any mention of the Divorce Court. She was pleasantly surprised to notice that her cousin blossomed out under the influence of David's gay personality and easy manner—Frances was presented in a totally new light and Sarah pondered on the difference brought about by the love that existed between Frances and David and which was so marked by the exchanged glances and intimate smiles and the tender atmosphere. She was happy for them and she refused to think about the unsatisfactory state of her own affairs for the time being.

But when she finally left them, tactfully removing her presence and returning to her hotel suite, she sank back against the cool leather upholstery of the taxi seat and her heart was heavy. She envied their confidence in the future, their unmistakable happiness and the love which flowed so obviously between them. Studying David and the attentions he paid to Frances, she realised only too clearly that he had never cared for her and although she was undisturbed emotionally by that fact, she was made a little despondent by the thought that she had never been able to inspire such evident devotion in his being. What did Frances possess that she lacked? Was it really true that only one man could inspire true love in a woman's heart and vice versa—or was it possible that one could be equally happy and as much in love with any of a dozen men depending on whichever of them entered one's life at a certain time? Sarah did not know the answer to the problem. She did know that she loved Andrew and needed his love desperately, that she had never felt so lonely as in the last two days since her marriage had broken up, that she could not bear to envisage the bleak, barren future which stretched before her without Andrew.

How foolish she had been! What a terrible mistake she had made in urging Andrew to marry her simply because she was gripped by an ephemeral passion for a man who had proved that he neither loved nor wanted her! Passion had blinded her to the realisation of the love that lived in her heart for Andrew—and the words of an old song filtered through her brain: "*Love is blind when passion rules!*" Well, the passion had faded and her heart's vision had cleared—but all too late. Her hopes of happiness with Andrew would never be fulfilled—and she turned her face abruptly away from the taxi-driver as she paid the fare so that he should not see the tears which welled in her eyes and threatened to spill . . .

14

ANDREW glanced up from the book he was reading at the announcement of Frances' name and put it aside with slow deliberation as she entered the library. He smiled a warm greeting and rose to his feet.

"Frances—how nice to see you! Did you enjoy your stay in London?" He stooped to kiss her cheek briefly. His words and gesture were almost mechanical: His first thought had been for Sarah and he wondered if Frances had brought him news of her.

Frances peeled off her gloves slowly, deliberately flashing the large sapphire and diamond ring she wore on the engagement finger of her left hand. But Andrew had turned away briefly and did not notice the ring or the ostentatious gesture of her hand.

"It's nice to be home again," she replied. "How are you, Andrew?"

"Fine," he assured her untruthfully. "Will you have some sherry?"

"No, thanks." She sat down and smiled at him. Surely he must notice the glow of excitement in her cheeks and the sparkle in her eyes even if he was blind to the symbol of happiness on her hand.

Andrew did notice the barely-subdued excitement but he had nothing with which to associate it so he made no mention of her high spirits. "Did you see Sarah again?" he asked, striving for casualness.

"Several times," she assured him. She met his eyes frankly. "She told me, Andrew," she added quietly.

He nodded, busying himself with the pouring of a drink. "It's unfortunate—but these things do happen. Sarah wasn't cut out to be the wife of a man like me, Frances. She's too restless, too volatile—and I'm just a little too dull for her, I suppose."

"That can't be true!" Frances protested. "You're not dull, Andrew."

He smiled. "Thanks for your support, anyway.

"Sarah will come back to you," Frances said. "I'm sure of that, Andrew."

"I doubt it," he said curtly and his tone implied that the subject was closed. "Tell me what you did with yourself in London, Frances—did you see any good shows? I suppose you've spent an alarming amount of money on clothes?"

"I've been living in a whirl," Frances said gaily.

He looked at her sharply, caught by the strikingly joyous tone of her voice. "You look radiant," he said slowly. "What happened?"

She held out her left hand to him. "I'm engaged, Andrew," she announced.

He caught her hand, studied the ring—and then searched her face intently. "I can't believe it," he said slowly. "Engaged? Do I know the man? I had no idea that you were even thinking of marriage, Frances."

She laughed. "I wasn't! I've been swept off my feet—and I'm getting married next week. It is incredible, isn't it? Sensible, cautious Frances Kendrick—oh, I can't believe it myself all the time. But it's true and I'm so happy, Andrew." She caught herself quickly. "Am I being tactless? You must be so upset about Sarah—and I come bursting in on you with my news."

He released her hand after a swift pressure. "I'm delighted with your news, Frances. But I'm still staggered by the shock—and it seems so sudden. It isn't my business, of course, but I've known you a long time, my dear, and I should hate you to make a mistake—you're quite sure you love this man and want to marry him so quickly?" His face clouded briefly. "It isn't always wise to rush into marriage, you know."

"Fools rush in?" she asked soberly. "I know, Andrew—but I *am* sure. I couldn't be so happy if I had any doubts."

"Now I must insist that you have a glass of sherry," he told her, turning to the decanters. "And I think I need another drink—you've taken my breath away. And you still haven't told me who it is that you're going to marry."

Frances hesitated—then plunged. "It's David Montrose, Andrew. You met him the other day when you drove me up to London—but you've heard of him several times, of course."

The decanter clattered against the glass.

He spun round and stared at her. "Montrose?" he echoed. She nodded. "But . . . I thought . . ."

"You thought he was in love with Sarah," she finished for him.

His jaw tightened. He turned back to the decanters and continued to pour out the drinks with a hand that was not quite steady. "Not exactly. Sarah led me to believe so, I will admit." He handed the glass to her. "Sarah knows of your engagement?"

"Yes, she does. And approves," Frances said firmly.

Andrew's mouth twisted. "She's scarcely in a position to disapprove or object, is she? At the risk of hurting you, Frances, I must say that Montrose seems to have let her down again—and I'm not very confident of your chances of happiness with him."

Frances flushed. "I am—and that's all that matters. I'm sorry you feel like that, Andrew. I think you're wrong about David—it may seem that he's let Sarah down but in actual fact he's done nothing of the kind. Oh, it's far too confusing to try to explain but I can assure you that

David loves me and I know we'll be happy." She smiled at him. "I knew the worst part would be telling you that David is the man I'm going to marry—but I hoped you'd be relieved."

"Why should I be relieved?" he asked, picking up a cigarette box from a table and offering it to her. Frances took a cigarette and received a light from him before she replied. "Now you and Sarah can patch things up," she said naively.

He looked at her steadily for a long moment. "So you imagined that Montrose was the only obstacle? I wish that were true. I wish it was only a case of a brief infatuation for another man, Frances— that I could forgive and forget. I'm afraid it goes much deeper, my dear, and the mere fact that you're going to marry David Montrose doesn't ease the situation at all."

"But Sarah doesn't love David," Frances pointed out.

"Neither does she love me," he returned firmly. "And that is the whole crux of the matter, Frances. It may well be that Sarah used Montrose in order to make me realise the hopelessness of our marriage—I've no idea how her mind works, I assure you.

You claim that she doesn't love Montrose —perhaps she does, perhaps she doesn't. I don't know one way or the other and it isn't likely that she would tell you the truth if she is in love with him. I know how she used to feel about him and that's enough for me. I've lived with her for over three months, my dear, and I've no reason to believe that her feelings have changed. I'm not prepared to go on living with a woman who doesn't care a damn for me— I've stifled my pride too much as it is. I should never have married Sarah in the first place . . . and I certainly shouldn't be telling you all this, anyway." He forced a smile. "You don't want to hear the details of an unhappy marriage, I know— certainly not when you're planning to be married yourself in a few days' time."

She drained the contents of her glass and laid it aside. "Andrew, I wish you'd see Sarah," she said slowly.

He raised an eyebrow. "What would be the purpose of seeing her?" he asked.

"Surely you could talk things over— come to some arrangement . . ."

"There's nothing to discuss," he interrupted shortly. "Sarah wants an annulment—and I'm prepared to fall in with her wishes. It's as simple as that Frances."

She was silent for a long moment. Then she sighed. "You know your own business best, of course. I shouldn't try to interfere. No doubt you and Sarah have made up your minds and talked it over—and nothing I can say or do will change things. But I'm so disappointed. I really thought you were happy together—and you're so well-suited, Andrew." Her tone was despondent.

He touched her cheek with an affectionate gesture. "Don't take it so seriously, Frances. It isn't the end of the world for either Sarah or me, you know. We lived our own lives before we were married— we've only three months to forget and it should be comparatively easy to pick up the old threads and kick over the traces. In any case, you're assuming that Sarah would be willing to come back to me—and I'm sure she has no thought or intention or desire to do so." A thought struck him and he added swiftly: "She doesn't seem to be unhappy, does she?"

Frances considered his question carefuliy. Then, reluctantly, she had to shake her head. "No, she doesn't. But I don't know, Andrew. She might be putting on a front—or she might not care a damn. I just don't know."

"Exactly. And Sarah is too transparent for there to be any doubt. You know her very well, Frances, after all. Surely you would know if she regretted the break-up of our marriage."

"I think I would," she had to admit.

"I appreciate your concern," he told her gently. "At the moment, it's natural for you to want everyone else to be as happy as you are—and you're reluctant to face the truth that sometimes a marriage doesn't work out. It hasn't with Sarah and myself. It was a gamble that didn't come off—and I knew the chances I was taking . . ."

"Then Sarah was still in love with David when she married you?" she asked, a tiny frown creasing her brow.

"Of course she was!" he returned curtly. "She must have played an excellent part to deceive you so well if you thought otherwise! She married me because Montrose made it obvious that he had no intention of marrying her—and she was hurt and angry. Her sole motive was to prove to him that he wasn't the only pebble on the beach—and possibly she hoped that he'd realise that he cared for her once she was married to someone else. You might as well know the whole truth, Frances. She refused to accept me as a husband because of that. We lived together as man and wife in name only and I promised that she should have her freedom at the end of a year if she was still in love with Montrose. I was mad to marry her—but I happened to love her and I thought I could wean her away from Montrose. As it happened, I was wrong. She may not love him any longer but she certainly doesn't welcome the idea of remaining married to me for the rest of her life!"

"If that is the truth, then you're better off without her," Frances said quietly.

"Oh, I agree," he returned swiftly. "That's why I'm going ahead with the annulment. I've loved Sarah for years but I managed to live without her for a very long time and I'm not losing very much anyway. Her friendship, of course—and I sincerely regret that. If I'd known real happiness during the last three months, I should be prepared to fight tooth and nail rather than give her up so easily—but I'd rather be without a wife than put up with the damnable torture of living as a stranger with the woman I love beyond anything." His tone was harsh and strained and Frances was shocked by the glimpse of primitive man which broke briefly through the thin veneer of civilisation in those few minutes. She was filled with pity for him, a great and stirring compassion, and she longed to put her arms about him and comfort him very much as she would have comforted a small child who was beginning to find life both bewildering and terrifying and uncertain. He turned away from the look in her eyes. "Sorry, Frances." He spoke smoothly, having swiftly regained his composure. "I've always found it easy to talk to you. But there are some secrets a man shouldn't divulge to anyone—and I hope you'll forget this conversation."

"I won't forget it," she returned gently, "but I won't repeat it to anyone, Andrew."

He turned to smile at her. "You're a loyal soul. And a very sweet person. I'd have done better to fall in love with you, Frances—but I suppose Montrose would still have beaten me to the tape."

Recalling the emotions he had once stirred in her being and the hopes she had once entertained in his direction, she coloured faintly and began to draw on her gloves, bending her head over the task with unnecessary attention to the smoothness of the soft kid. She rose to her feet. "I must go. I haven't been home yet. I came straight here to tell you about my engagement to David."

His eyes were warm. "In the hope that it would solve the problem of Sarah and myself? Thank you, Frances—I'm only sorry that the solution isn't so easy." He went to her and placed his hands on her shoulders. "Be happy, my dear," he said tenderly. "One word of warning—don't expect too much of marriage no matter how much you love the man you marry. He's only human, after all—with the faults and failings of every human being. If he loves you—and he'd be a fool if he didn't —then you're very fortunate because marriage is nothing without love, I assure you." He kissed her cheek and smoothed a strand of hair from her brow. "I won't keep you any longer. You must be bursting to tell Sarah's parents."

She looked up at him. "They know about you and Sarah?"

He spread his hands. "I don't know. I haven't told them. I've been avoiding them all the week. Sarah might have telephoned them—I expect she has, in fact. But I preferred to say nothing in case Sarah came home unexpectedly—and I admit I've been hoping that she would."

"Then you would take her back, despite everything?"

Again his voice took on that note of harshness. "Of course I would—if she came back of her own volition. When you love someone as much as I love Sarah, you forgive anything—and put up with anything. But I don't think I need to tell you that, Frances," he added on a quieter note. "I can see that you're very much in love with David Montrose—and I only hope that he comes up to your expectations."

"He loves me and that's all I ask," she said and the humility of her voice struck him forcibly.

He nodded. "That's all anyone wants—to be loved."

When she had gone, he threw himself into his former chair and closed his eyes. How wise Frances was—to demand nothing of the man she was going to marry except that he should love her as she loved him. If he had been as wise and as perceptive, he would not be in the hellish position that he was now. He had been so confident of winning Sarah's love, so convinced that eventually she would allow him to take Montrose's place in her heart —the vanity of a man in love! Marriage should never be entered into unless there was mutual love—it was far too serious a thing to be treated lightly. Love did not come knocking on the door after the marriage vows had been made purely as a matter of course: it either had to be very much in evidence beforehand or else the initial seeds of love must already be planted; and in his marriage to Sarah, neither had been the case. He had hoped for a miracle!

He had persuaded himself that because they had many mutual interests, a similar background, a friendship of long standing and a warm affection for each other, they also had every chance of being happy in their marriage. He had overlooked the vital point which Frances had perceived with her instinctive feminine intuition: that if he and Sarah had loved each other, the other things would have been unimportant; they would have discovered or created mutual interests, background would not have mattered, friendship and affection would have sprung from their love for each other. Frances and David Montrose might be comparative strangers yet they loved each other and Andrew was willing to assert with every confidence that they were assured of a successful and happy marriage because of that one possession. It had not been enough that he loved Sarah—from the very beginning he had resented her inability to love him in return and expected too much of the life they shared.

He had promised to be patient for a year —yet he had swiftly leaped to conclusions when he found David Montrose with Sarah in her hotel suite and just as swiftly he had announced his intention to have their marriage annulled. It had taken only three months for his patience to run out, for his pride to take precedence over his love—yet surely he could not be blamed. Sarah had made it only too obvious that he would never ignite the flame of love in her being: she had deliberately contacted David Montrose at her first opportunity; she had made no attempt to excuse her behaviour and certainly she had not pleaded for another chance or tried to persuade him to change his mind. She had accepted his decision with apparent calmness and he had no reason to doubt that she was in full agreement.

As he had pointed out to Frances, whether or not Sarah still cared for David Montrose was immaterial and irrelevant—the crux of the matter was that she definitely did not care for him and showed no signs of doing so in the future therefore he had no alternative but to secure freedom for them both from the bonds of a marriage that was intolerable and unsuccessful.

Freedom could only bring relief for them both: it would release him from the anguish and strain of living with Sarah and loving her desperately yet knowing the futility of his love and the emptiness of their marriage; and it must release her from the knowledge of guilt that she could not respond to his love for her—she was a sensitive woman and it must have been difficult for her during the last few months to live with him, aware of his feelings and the restraint he placed upon himself, yet knowing that she was incapable of responding to those feelings or easing the restraint.

He must not blame Sarah too much. Love could not be forced and it was not her fault if he lacked the vital spark which would ignite the flame of love. No doubt she regretted the state of affairs. It was possible that there had been times when she wished with all her heart that she could love him, when the failure of their marriage caused her pain and regret, when she thought about the future and wished it were possible that she would not have to hurt him by asking for her eventual freedom.

No, he did not blame Sarah. Because he loved her so desperately and so deeply, it was easy to absolve her from blame. He should never have encouraged her to follow that ridiculous impulse which led her to ask him to marry her. He should never have allowed matters to go any further and certainly he should have pointed out that it would be absolute folly to risk their happiness on such an uncertain foundation for marriage. He should have realised that only disappointment, pain and bitterness could come of a marriage in which love was so totally one-sided. Certainly he should have insisted on a six month engagement during which time it would have become evident whether or not Sarah was ever likely to forget David Montrose and fall in love with him.

So much pain and heartache could have been prevented . . .

If only he had realised how important it was to be loved . . .

15

SARAH knew the relief of a brief respite when she arrived to find that Andrew was out and was not expected home until the evening.

She had summoned all her courage and made up her mind to ask Andrew if there was any chance of making a fresh start. She was prepared to humble her pride and to do all in her power to atone for the hurt and humiliation she had brought him if only she could know once more the security and comfort of sharing his life. The past few days had served to emphasise the bleak emptiness of life without him and although, at first, she had been determined that nothing would induce her to make such an appeal to him her loneliness and her need of him had won the battle over her pride.

She went into the library and looked about the large, comfortable and vaguely masculine room. It was empty yet it managed to remind her vividly of Andrew:

the pile of papers lying on the desk, his fountain pen, the cigarette lighter he had evidently forgotten, a crumpled newspaper thrown into an armchair and an empty glass standing on a small table beside an ashtray which contained several cigarette stubs. She stood in the middle of the room and ran a hand through her auburn curls in a characteristic gesture . . .

Andrew would be astonished to find her at the house—would he also be displeased? If only he would ask no questions—simply hold out his arms to her with a smile of welcome and love shining in his eyes. How swiftly she would run to him and how happy she would be to rest her head on his shoulder and know the strong clasp of his arms and the reassurance of his love. She sighed briefly. It was nice to day-dream but remembering the steel of his dark eyes and the cold finality of his spoken decision to arrange an annulment of their marriage it was futile to indulge in flights of fancy until she discovered his reaction to her presence. She had no idea what she would say to him, how she would broach the subject of their marriage—but during the journey back to Avering from

London, she had determined that it was better not to mentally prepare her appeal but to allow events to take their natural course once she was with him.

Should she tell him that she loved him? Was it likely that he would believe her? By now, he must surely know of Frances' engagement to David and it was natural enough that he should leap to the conclusion that Sarah had returned to him only because David had once again disappointed her. Or so it would seem to him and Sarah could not bear the thought of the contempt which would flash into his expression if she dared to speak of the love which she had so lately recognised for herself. It was a horrible mix-up and she was tense, almost distraught, with the fear that Andrew would turn her away. How could she possibly make him understand that her life was nothing without him, that she needed him and the safe harbour of their marriage, that she deeply regretted all that had happened in the last few days and wished with all her heart that it was possible to turn back the pages and erase the misunderstanding and folly

267

which marred the contentment they had once known.

Slowly, she walked from the library and made her way up the wide staircase to her bedroom. If her appeal failed then she would return to London on the following day—and so certain was she of the hopelessness of her mission, that she occupied the next hour or so with sorting through her wardrobe and dressing-table drawers and neatly packing various clothes into her travelling cases. It gave her something to think about but her thoughts continually strayed from her task: such a few months ago, she had been carefully packing her clothes and personal possessions preparatory to moving into Andrew's charming old house as his wife. It had been a short-lived interlude but one which would always remain in her memory as a few months of remarkable happiness. It was surprising that she had been so lacking in perception. She had called the quiet peace of her being "contentment" and called the harmonious relationship which she shared with Andrew "affection". Only now did she realise that she had never been so happy in her life as during those three months of marriage with Andrew and that the quiet intimacy and peace of mind and sense of belonging owed itself to the love she knew for her husband which she was unable to recognise until her happiness lay in shattered pieces at her feet . . .

The afternoon became evening and the rays of sunlight slanted unevenly across the bedroom carpet. Sarah curled up in a cat-like attitude on the window-seat and gazed across the well-planned and carefully-cultivated gardens which her bedroom window overlooked. Glancing at her watch, she told herself that if Andrew meant to be home in time to change for dinner he must soon return—and her heart began to race with trepidation and anticipation. She fought down the impulse to take her packed cases and slip away before he came home. She had made up her mind to see him and talk to him and now that she had come this far, she would stay and see things through. Only cowards ran away at the last minute—and cowardice had never been one of her failings. Indeed, she was reckless in the extreme and her lack of caution combined with her wild impulses had led her into many foolish escapades in the past—but none so foolish as persuading Andrew to marry her and again a brief sigh escaped her lips. She had taken advantage of his love and the knowledge that he had always hoped to marry her: she had used him without a thought for his feelings or for the future; because of this, they had both suffered and it seemed more than likely that she would continue to pay for her folly for a long time to come. If Andrew had really ceased to love her, then he was fortunate because he could view the future with equanimity and indifference to the failure of their marriage. But she loved him and she would always love him and she could not visualise a time when any other man would manage to erase the memory of her happiness with Andrew and her self-induced pain and regret that she had lost his love and his trust and his friendship . . .

Suddenly she stiffened. Andrew's tall, familiar figure was striding through the gardens to the house. He was casually dressed in tan slacks and thick blue sweater, a cravat at his throat. He walked swiftly and purposefully and her heart swelled with love for him as she watched his unswerving approach. Did he sense her watching eyes? How could he remain so unaware of the love which flowed from her being? Tense, unconsciously breathing a silent prayer, she willed him to glance up at her bedroom window—but he gazed directly before him and within a few moments was lost to sight as he turned the corner of the house. Sarah's body slumped —and only then did she realise how tense had been her position and how vitally important it had been that he should become aware of her presence. Foolishly, she had persuaded herself that if he looked up then it would mean that everything was going to be all right—but if he walked on without a glance then it was a sign of impending failure. Her heart was heavy as she rose from the window seat and moved towards the dressing-table. Listlessly, she ran a brush through her curls and swiftly gave her nose a dusting of powder. She would be wasting her time but she would go down to him and make her appeal . . . She had nothing to lose, after all—for she had already lost everything that mattered to her—and there was still the slender

271

thread of hope which she could not entirely suppress.

Softly, she closed the bedroom door behind her and heard the sound of Andrew's voice as he talked to the manservant in the hall. Her heart was thumping painfully and her lips were dry. She moistened her lips with the tip of her small, pink tongue and rubbed the palms of her hands down her skirt to remove the perspiration which had suddenly broken out all over her. She stood still, frozen by the trepidation which gripped at the pit of her stomach and turned her blood to ice in the veins. Would she find all the right words? It was so important that he should know how sincere she was—one false word, the wrong expression in her eyes, one hasty movement could mean failure. She finally found enough strength in legs that seemed weak and rubbery to walk to the head of the staircase. Gripping the wooden balustrade with both hands, she looked over and saw Andrew standing in the hall. At that moment, he looked up —apparently in response to something his manservant said to him—and Sarah saw the look of incredulity which crossed his features. Then he nodded curtly to the servant and walked to the foot of the stairs.

For a moment, they stood looking at each other. She saw no encouragement in his eyes, nothing but a cold appraisal, and a swift stab of pain caught her heart and pierced the innermost depths of her being.

Quietly, but in a tone that carried clearly, he said: "You'd better come down, Sarah. I'll be in the library." He turned on his heel and strode across the hall. He did not close the library door and Sarah could hear the faint chink of decanters as she slowly descended the staircase, her brain suddenly numb as she frenziedly tried to think of something to say to him and hastily tried to recall why she had come to see him!

She closed the library door and stood with her back against the panels. He turned to look at her briefly then he continued to pour out the soft amber sherry. He held out the glass to her and Sarah pulled herself together. She walked across the thick carpet and took the glass from his hand. "Thank you, Andrew." She was surprised that her voice did not falter and that she found it remarkably easy to speak his name without a tremor.

"You came to collect your things, I suppose," he said coolly. "I'm sorry I disturbed you. Are you staying at Kendrick House tonight?"

"I doubt it," she replied. "I came to see you, Andrew—not to collect my things."

He glanced at her sharply. "I see. You're not sure about one or two points and you want to discuss them?"

She smiled. "Stop leaping to conclusions. As soon as I've tasted my drink, I'll tell you why I'm here."

"Sorry—I'm rushing you." He moved to scoop the newspaper from the armchair. "Sit down, Sarah." He offered her a cigarette when she was seated and fumbled in his trouser pocket for his lighter.

"Your lighter's on the desk," she told him.

"Oh, thanks." He stretched out a hand to pick it up and flicked the lighter into flame. Sarah bowed her head and drew deeply on her cigarette. Throwing back her head, she exhaled the smoke in a grateful sigh—and wondered why she should now feel so composed where only a few minutes previously she had been trembling and uncertain and afraid to face Andrew. Perhaps it was the very reassurance of his familiar features, the broad shoulders which implied in some strange way the strength of his character, the ease with which she could for a brief moment persuade herself that the events of the past few days had been nothing but a nightmare and that they were sharing a pre-dinner sherry and cigarette in the accustomed manner.

He leaned against the edge of his desk and folded his arms across his chest, regarding her thoughtfully. She studied the amber liquid in her glass which she swirled absently in the silence which had fallen—not a difficult, embarrassing silence but a momentary interlude during which words were not necessary as a communion between two human beings who had always been very close friends.

Andrew had been taken aback to find her at the house—yet in the next moment he had asked himself why he should be so amazed. In his heart, he had known that she would come back and although there was nothing in her manner or expression to confirm it, he did not need to ask what she was doing in the home they had shared since their marriage. She had come back to him—and he did not mean to question too closely the gift the Gods had sent. It was sufficient that she had returned of her own free will and he did not want to enquire into her motives. Perhaps there was some hope for the future, after all. It could well be that once again she had turned to him as a solace for her disappointment in David Montrose—but because he loved her he would take her back on any terms!

Sarah knocked ash from her cigarette and came directly to the point. "Andrew, do you want to end our marriage?"

He parried the thrust cautiously: "Are you trying to say that you've changed your mind?"

"It was *your* decision," she reminded him adroitly.

He conceded that point with a slight dip of his head. "Agreed—but it seemed obvious that you wanted your freedom."

A slight colour stained her cheeks. But she lifted her chin swiftly. "You're referring to my meeting with David Montrose, of course."

"Montrose or any other man," he said sharply. "The inference would be the same, Sarah. A contented wife doesn't make arrangements to meet former men friends without her husband's knowledge."

"I'm willing to admit that I was in the wrong," Sarah said quietly. "If you'd given me time to apologise . . ."

"Apologies are of no use to me," he interrupted her swiftly. "I want a loyal wife—I thought that was understood when we were married." He paused briefly and then went on, unable to stem the hurtful words: "I'm not prepared to put up with a wife who thinks she can be unfaithful one day and come running back to me the next!"

She placed her glass on the table by her side with a sharp little sound of rejection. "I've never been unfaithful to you, Andrew!"

"I'm glad to hear that," he said sincerely. "But the existence of the thought doesn't cancel out the failure of the deed, Sarah."

"You're being pompous," she told him, anxiety making her tone irritable. "Do I have to remind you again that it's fatal to leap to conclusions?"

He raised an eyebrow. "All right, Sarah —one question which I hope you'll answer honestly. If Montrose had urged you to leave me and live with him—would you have done so?"

Sarah hesitated. Did Andrew know that David had already made that suggestion to her even if he regretted it immediately? Had Frances seen him and told him what had transpired between David and herself? How could she reply with full honesty that before Andrew's arrival at the hotel in London she would have considered accepting David's proposal but that only a few hours later she had realised that her only happiness lay with the man she had married?

Andrew took her hesitation and long silence for confirmation of his suspicion. His eyes were cold and hard as he looked at her, disappointment filling him to the exclusion of his love in that moment. "I see," he said quietly. "So I have Montrose to thank for your unexpected return.

Because he is going to marry Frances, you've decided that you might as well continue to live with me and suffer all the unpleasantness and frustration of a marriage that failed before it really began."

"No!" The exclamation was forced from her. "Andrew—that isn't true! Of course it seems like that to you. I can understand that! But David has nothing to do with my being here now."

He raised an eyebrow in a gesture of incredulity. "I find that very hard to accept, Sarah."

All the fight seeped from her being and she leaned against the back of the armchair, suddenly tired and despondent and knowing a great indifference to the outcome of it all which owed itself to the heaviness of her heart. "I can't blame you," she said slowly. "All right, Andrew—there's nothing else to say, is there? I hoped you'd be willing to give our marriage another chance but you're not and it was stupid of me to think that you might still care a little for me."

He took an involuntary step forward— and then checked the movement. "Is that so important to you, Sarah?" he asked quietly.

She met his eyes levelly. "Yes, it is."

"Why?"

She moved her slim shoulders in a tiny shrug. "I've always been able to rely on your affection, Andrew. I feel very lost without it."

He was silent for a moment. Then he said: "I'm still very fond of you, Sarah. I'm afraid old habits die hard with me. I can't forget the years of friendship just like that, you know. No matter what you did, I would always think of you with affection—I'm surprised that you should doubt that."

She searched his expression and found sincerity—and her spirits revived faintly. If he was still fond of her—if their friendship survived despite everything—then surely there was some hope for the future! She would not ask that he love her—she would be humble and grateful for the smallest sign of his affection—she would be patient and concentrate on giving fully of her love and in the meantime she could surely hope that his love for her was not completely extinct!

"Then—can't we try again, Andrew?" she asked and she strove to keep eagerness from her voice, something within her warning that she must not try too hard for what she wanted, that she must accept the tempo which he chose to apply to their relationship in future.

He pulled thoughtfully at his chin, looking down at the carpet. "Is it worth it, Sarah?" he asked in return. "Do you honestly believe that we can salvage anything from our marriage? God knows it had little enough chance at the beginning —now it would have even less."

"We were happy, Andrew," she told him and her hands were clenched together so tightly that her finger-nails dug tiny crescents into the palms.

His mouth twisted wryly. "Were we?"

"I was much happier than I thought possible," she insisted.

He glanced at her with narrowed eyes. 'I believed you were fairly happy, I admit —until the other day and then I knew I'd been living in a fool's paradise." He turned away from her and moved over to the decanters. "All right we'll assume that you were happy," he went on as he poured fresh drinks into their glasses. "Did you think I was happy too—under the circumstances?"

Sarah bit her lip at his question. "I've never been fair to you, Andrew," she admitted honestly. "I expected far too much of you—and I'm sorry. If you'll try again, I promise that it will be different this time. It won't be a marriage on approval. We won't always have the thought that at the end of a year we'll have to discuss the future hanging over our heads. We'll try to make a real marriage. We could start a family, if you wished— oh, Andrew, it is worth trying again."

He nodded. "It sounds as though you mean it, Sarah—but I wonder how long it will be before you change your mind again."

"You will take me back?" she asked, ignoring the latter part of his sentence.

He handed her glass over to her. "I'm willing to take a chance. I've always had an aversion to failure in anything I undertake. But I don't think we'll start a family, Sarah—at least, not until I'm convinced that our marriage will last long enough to provide a family atmosphere for a child."

He drank his own sherry and moved towards the door. "Now I must change for dinner. I'd better tell them to lay your place . . ."

"I've already done so," she told him swiftly.

He looked over his shoulder—and then his mouth relaxed into amusement. "You were very sure of yourself, Sarah."

She shook her head. "No—but I knew you wouldn't refuse to feed me even if you refused to support me any longer." She smiled at him tremulously. Then, suddenly, she rose to her feet and ran to him, putting her arms about him. "Andrew—forgive me," she pleaded.

He stiffened. He let his arms remain by his sides but he suffered her embrace until she sensed the lack of response, the coldness within him, then she released him and moved away, only the striking pallor of her cheeks betraying the pain which swept through her in that moment.

"I'm sorry—that wasn't such a good idea," she said stiffly and kept her face averted so he should not see the acute misery in her eyes and the trembling of her lips which she could not control.

Momentarily, he longed to catch her into his arms, to beg her forgiveness for rebuffing her impulsive gesture of the olive-branch, to kiss her until animation returned to those dead eyes and stiff features—but he had given too generously of his love in the past and he would not open his heart so swiftly again to hurt and humiliation. Without a word, he opened the library door and left the room.

16

SARAH caught sight of Frances and David in the distance and waved to them as she turned the corner of the lane. Her mount moved with graceful rhythm beneath her slim body and her cheeks were flushed with the whipping of the wind. Her auburn curls were dishevelled and rioting about her well-shaped head.

She reached them and drew her horse to a halt. Restless, he chafed beneath the restraining rein and she ran her hand lightly over his neck as she smiled down at Frances. "Hullo! I didn't know you were in Avering."

"We only arrived this afternoon," Frances told her. She hugged David's arm and he glanced down at her with love in his eyes.

"How are you, Sarah?" he asked.

"Fine," she replied lightly. "How's married life?"

"Wonderful!" Frances answered.

"Sarah, I'm going to have a baby!" There could be no doubt of her happiness as she made the tremulous, excited announcement and the look she flashed at her husband caused envy to spark in Sarah's breast.

"That is good news," Sarah returned warmly. "I'm so pleased. How do you view the thought of being a father, David?"

He grinned. "Surprisingly enough, I'm as pleased as Frances. I suppose you can't imagine me as a family man?"

Sarah laughed. "I could never imagine you as a married man, quite frankly—but you seem to be happy enough. When do you go back to London? I hope you'll be down here long enough to dine with us one evening."

"I shall be over to see Andrew tomorrow," Frances said swiftly. "We'll talk about it then, Sarah, shall we?"

Sarah nodded, a shadow flitting briefly across her eyes. "Yes, of course." Again the horse moved impatiently beneath her and she added hastily: "I must get on— I'm late for dinner now. I'm really thrilled with your news, Frances. We'll see you tomorrow then?"

She left them and cantered briskly along the lane, glancing back once to wave gaily. They were strolling hand in hand and Frances was talking animatedly to David who looked down at her with a fond expression—they had already dismissed Sarah from their minds and did not notice her wave of farewell. She gave the horse his head and he carried her homewards, knowing his way, while she stared ahead with sadness in the curve of her mouth and in the depths of her eyes. She envied her cousin's happiness and the love which flowed so unmistakably between Frances and David. The news that Frances was going to have a child had touched a tender note. Their child would seal the happiness of their marriage—and Sarah wished desperately that Andrew would consent to her appeal for a child. They had been married for nine months and they still lived together as strangers—but now it was Andrew who made no attempt to consummate their marriage and Sarah was too proud to admit openly that she loved him and would welcome the passion which he kept so strictly under control.

It seemed incredible that six months had passed since they began their second attempt at building a successful marriage —the time had passed swiftly enough, it was true, but it seemed he could not forgive her disloyalty and she was incapable of bringing back to life the love he had once known for her. Outwardly, they were happy together—but only Sarah and Andrew knew the loss of the intimacy which they had shared in the first three months of their marriage. Even their long friendship had apparently foundered and there were many times when Sarah told herself that they were wasting their lives, that they would never know real happiness, that her love for him would never evoke any response and that they should have done the wisest thing and parted when the break had been imminent.

She thought of Frances' swift avoidance of accepting her invitation that she and David should dine with them one evening —and it reminded her vividly that Andrew and David had made no attempt to forget the past and create a friendship. The two men had met from time to time but nothing could ease the cold formality and hostility which existed between them. Apart from anything else, a mutual dislike was very much in evidence. It was fortunate that Frances and David lived in London and only made brief visits to Avering: once or twice, Sarah had gone up to Town and met her cousin and David: occasionally, when they came down to Avering, she and Andrew had been invited to dinner at Kendrick House and on one unforgettable occasion, Sarah had instigated a small dinner party of her own to which Frances and David had been invited —Andrew had been stiff and formal, making no effort to ease the atmosphere and oblivious to Sarah's rising anger, and eventually Frances had pleaded a headache in order to escape from the embarrassment of the evening.

Sarah was never troubled by thoughts of David. She had dismissed him completely from her heart and memory and merely accepted him as her cousin's husband. All her thoughts and emotions were occupied by her love for Andrew—a hopeless love but one that remained as strong as ever and which clung to the slender thread of the love he had once known for her and which might one day be resurrected if only she could be patient and understanding. She would be generous with her love, too, if only Andrew would give her the opportunity but he continued to rebuff any affectionate advances on her part and slowly she was finding it more and more difficult to be demonstrative towards him. Whenever the impulse to put her arms around him or lean over to kiss his cheek or brow or stretch out a hand to clasp his strong, brown fingers seized her she invariably repressed it these days, remembering how often he had stood immobile in her arms, how frequently he had turned away his head to avoid her kisses, how seldom he allowed his hand to remain beneath hers for longer than a brief moment before he moved it from her touch.

She had been blind and foolish—but she had paid in full with pain and tears and desperate longing. Surely life would not continue to be so cruel. Surely soon Andrew would relent. He had assured her that whatever happened she would retain his affection—was it possible that he could be fond of her still and never betray his feelings, that he could subdue all his impulses of affection and passion, that he could never know a momentary response to the love which burned within her and which he must surely suspect by now?

She reached the house and dismounted. Walking round to the stables, she handed over her horse to a groom and entered the house a few minutes later by way of the open library window. Andrew glanced up as she came into the room and nodded a brief greeting.

"I saw Frances and David in the lane," she said without preliminary.

"I was with your father when they arrived this morning," he told her absently, concentrating on filling in a portion of the crossword which occupied his attention. "We were invited to dinner tomorrow night but I explained that we had another engagement."

"But that isn't true, Andrew," Sarah said quickly.

He looked up. "I know but I dislike the effort of exchanging social chit-chat with Montrose and I hate to see Frances hanging on his every word as though the man were a gift from the gods."

"They're very much in love," Sarah told him sharply. She pulled off her gloves and took a cigarette from the box on the table. Absently he handed her his lighter and she lighted her cigarette. "I'm sorry you feel incapable of accepting David," she went on. "Sometimes I think it would be generous of you to make the attempt."

"Montrose can manage very well without my generosity," he told her curtly. "Did you enjoy your ride?" he asked, trying to switch the subject to more pleasant things.

"Frances is going to have a baby," she told him, ignoring his question.

He put aside his newspaper. "All right, Sarah—get it off your chest," he said with a little sigh.

She gestured impatiently with the hand that held her cigarette. "Andrew—why won't you be reasonable? Is it asking so much of you to let me have a child? Will we never have a normal married life?" She began to pace the room restlessly. "I can't stand much more of this," she said and her voice shook. "Andrew—our marriage is in a worse state now than it was six months ago! You knew that I was willing to make a completely new start—to live with you properly—to have a normal marriage like everyone else! Do you hate me so much now? Can't you even bear to kiss me?" Her voice rose with a note of hysteria and he rose swiftly to his feet. Catching her by the shoulders, he swung her round to face him.

"That's enough, Sarah!" he said sharply. "Just because you've seen Montrose again—and you can't stand the truth that he's happy with Frances—there isn't any need to pretend that our marriage is on the rocks because I won't let you have a child. You're jealous of Frances—that's all it is . . ."

"Jealous!" she repeated—and then she laughed. It was a hollow, bitter sound completely lacking in humour. "Yes, I'm jealous of Frances—not because she's going to have a baby but because her husband's in love with her!"

He stared down at her—and saw the naked desperation in her eyes, the months of weary pain and longing and futile love written clearly for him to see for the first time. "Sarah . . ."

She wrenched her shoulders from the hands which had tightened involuntarily. She lifted her chin and faced him defiantly. "Well, Andrew?"

"Sarah, don't torment me!" he warned her harshly and his voice was like a whiplash.

"What do *you* know of torment?" she cried. "*You* haven't waited six months for one word of affection, one unsought embrace, one brief touch of the hand. . . !" Her eyes filled with tears and she turned her head away swiftly.

His hand was firm on her chin, hurting her, as he brought her face round again. "I didn't know," he said slowly. "I swear I didn't know . . ."

"Did you want me to shout it from the roof?" she asked him bitterly. "What was I supposed to do, Andrew? I've tried to show you in a hundred ways how much I love you—and you've treated me like a casual acquaintance who happens to live in the same house!"

"Sarah!" he said and the word was a groan. "I wouldn't hurt you for the world

—not deliberately! I didn't know—how could I know? A dozen times I've hoped and every time I've called myself all kinds of a fool for daring to imagine that you might love me. It's so easy to deceive oneself, to hope when there's no foundation for hope, to read all sorts of things into the smallest gesture of affection. I've been tormented too, Sarah—loving you so much and thinking that everything was just as hopeless as ever."

A tear welled from her eye and ran slowly down her cheek. "Then you do love me?" The words were a mere whisper.

For answer, he gently brushed away the tear with his hand and kissed the cheek it had traced with wetness. A sob rose up in her and caught in her throat. The next moment she was crushed against his chest and his cheek was hard and firm against her small head with its crop of silken curls.

"For God's sake, darling—don't cry!" he said painfully. "I can't bear it if you cry. All I wanted was to make you happy —and I didn't even do that!"

With the realisation of his distress, her own tears subsided and she was suddenly calm and strengthened as a woman is always strengthened in moments of tense emotion. Her arms held him close and her love flowed over him in silent reassurance and comfort.

At last, he drew away and looked down into her small, lovely face. "Sarah—what happens now?" he asked.

She smiled tremulously. "We try again —for the third time. But this time we'll start off on an equal footing. This time we'll know that we love each other—you do love me, Andrew?" she added urgently, desperately.

His eyes were warm and glowing with the vibrant assurance of his love. "More than I've ever loved you," he told her gently.

Her sigh was one of contentment as she laid her head on his shoulder. "I thought you stopped loving me six months ago," she said and the remembrance of all she had suffered gave a hint of sadness to her voice.

He touched her hair with his lips. "I'd never do that, darling—no matter what happened. I thought I made that clear at the time."

She shook her head. "You said you'd always be fond of me," she said firmly.

He smiled and kissed her forehead where the curls sprang vitally away from the hairline. "A poor choice of words, I admit. I should have told you then that I still loved you more than anything else in the world—that you were my whole life."

"It would have saved an awful lot of misunderstanding," Sarah said quietly. "But I shouldn't have been so proud. When I asked you for another chance, I should have been honest enough to tell you that I loved you and couldn't face the future without you."

"My own pride would probably have prevented me from believing you, darling," he murmured and kissed the long, dark lashes which still sparkled from the recent tears.

"That's why I couldn't tell you," she whispered. "For years I'd been running eagerly to you every time I thought I was in love. You knew how stupidly infatuated I was with David—and at the time I did think I loved him. I was afraid that you'd never believe me if I told you that I really loved you and that I'd never loved anyone else—it would have been like the little boy who cried wolf!"

"I might have been too willing to believe you—and known another disappointment," he reminded her and his lips strayed along the clear-cut, beautiful line of her cheek.

"You believe me now, Andrew?" she asked anxiously. "I love you—so very much."

"I believe you," he assured her. "I love you, Sarah—with all my heart." His lips touched the warm, sweet curve of her mouth and he knew the eager response which convinced him now and forever that he need never again doubt her love.

DOM

Library at Home Service
Community Services
Hounslow Library, CentreSpace
24 Treaty Centre, High Street
Hounslow TW3 1ES

YOUR COMMUNITY
YOUR SERVICES

0	1	2	3	4	5	6	7	8	9
535↑			553		525	630	887		929
240			513		995	706	367	378	9529
970			993			307 86	507	638	
	861					16		818	
						2606	7427	9578	
						3087			
						3457			
						346	3497		

P10-L-2061